OTHER YEARLING BOOKS YOU WILL ENJOY:

RATS, SPIDERS, & LOVE

BONNIE PRYOR

Illustrated by
J. Winslow Higginbottom

A Yearling Book

Published by
Dell Publishing
a division of
The Bantam Doubleday Dell Publishing Group, Inc.
666 Fifth Avenue
New York, New York 10103

ISBN: 0-440-40138-0

Reprinted by arrangement with William Morrow and Company, Inc.

Printed in the United States of America

February 1989

10 9 8 7 6 5 4 3 2 1

CW

To my dad…
B.P.

For Wayne, Billy, and Vaughn -
who understand…
J.W.H.

Contents

A Big Zero

~

"If I hear one more person say how pretty my sister Julie is," Samantha announced, "I may throw up."

"Well, you have to admit she is pretty," her best friend Sara Rubens answered. "But I think you are, too," she added loyally. "If you would fix your hair a little, and dress up sometimes, you would be just as pretty."

Sam ran her fingers through her straight brown hair, shook out the sand, and picked up her towel. "That's easy for you to say. At least you've got something to work with."

She looked at her friend's dark wavy hair and brown eyes and sighed. "I've got to get home and start something for dinner," she said as she got up

2

from the beach. "It's almost five, and Mom will be home soon."

"You are so lucky. I wish my Mom would let me cook," Sara said with a trace of envy in her voice. "My Mom won't let me near the kitchen when she is cooking. Says it makes her nervous to have someone watching. All I get to do is the dishes."

"You wouldn't think it was so great if you had to do it all the time. Besides, I don't get to do any of the good stuff. All I do is peel potatoes and set the table. Mom does the cooking when she gets home from work."

"I guess I might as well go home, too," Sara sighed. "It's no fun here alone. I'm glad I had a few minutes of peace and quiet. I have to watch my little brother tonight while my parents go out."

"I wish I had your little brother instead of Julie and Kevin," Sam said. "It must be nice to be the oldest. I wouldn't even mind being the youngest."

"It's not as terrific as you think. I have to watch Jeremy all the time when my parents go out. And for free. At least if I was baby-sitting for someone else, I would get paid."

"I wouldn't mind watching him. I think he's cute."

"That's what you think. He has decided he doesn't want to eat. Everything you give him he throws on the floor and says it's yucky. Mom keeps saying it's just a stage, and he will grow out of it, but I'm embarrassed to have anyone come over. They might get a plate of food in their lap."

"Maybe you should invite all your enemies," Sam giggled. She waved good-bye. "I'd still trade," she called back as she trudged up the well-worn path to her house.

Sara's house was around the cove in a new housing development called Seal Point. The houses there were large and elegant with sloping lawns and a retaining wall to hold back the sand and salt as they fought to gain a few more inches. Beautiful as the Seal Point houses were, Sam wouldn't have traded one of them for her own weatherbeaten house perched on stilts on a hill directly above the Pacific Ocean. The house had turned a soft, faded gray on the outside, but inside it was warm and cozy. It had held its precarious position for nearly fifty years, which was more than you could say for the newer houses along the beach. Sam loved every inch of the house's worn boards.

When her father was living, it had been the family's summer home. But her mother had not been able to keep up the expenses on their large house in Portland. She had sold it and moved Sam and her brother and sister to the beach. It was a move that suited Sam to a tee. From her bedroom window she could look out over the water. Often at night, leaning her chin on her arms and gazing out over the ocean, she could see the faint lights of passing ships heading to some unknown port. Sam liked to imagine the exotic places they might be heading, but not with envy. She was content right where she was. At night she slept lulled by the pounding waves. Mornings she walked on the beach looking for small treasures deposited by the tide. It was, she thought, the best place in the world to live.

Mrs. Wilson, who lived next door, gaily waved as they passed on the path. On her head was perched the gigantic hat she always wore to the beach.

"A girl must watch her complexion," Mrs. Wilson was fond of saying. That always made Samatha smile. Mrs. Wilson was nearly sixty—hardly a girl—and she weighed close to two hundred pounds. She painted pictures of the ocean and sold them to the tourists in Glen Harbor. Mrs. Wilson was always smiling and friendly, and she was one of Sam's favorite people.

"Going home so early?" Mrs. Wilson stopped to ask.

"I have to start dinner," Sam replied.

"Your mother is such a lucky woman," Mrs. Wilson beamed. "To have three such wonderful children. I hear that brother of yours won a scholarship at the university next year. And Julie is so pretty, it almost takes your breath away. And you always helping like you do. She is one lucky woman."

Good old reliable me, Sam thought grimly. But she smiled at Mrs. Wilson and waved. "Gotta go. See you later, Mrs. Wilson."

"Wait. You haven't heard my riddle," Mrs. Wilson exclaimed.

"All right. But only one. I'm already late," Sam grinned. She couldn't remember how it had started, but every day for as long as she could remember, Mrs. Wilson had told her a riddle.

"If there were three fat ladies under one regular-size umbrella, why didn't any of them get wet?"

Sam chuckled. "I know that one. Because it wasn't raining."

Mrs. Wilson pretended to pout. "Oh, dear. You are getting too good. I'll have to find some harder ones."

Mrs. Wilson continued down the path, juggling her paints and easel. Sam smiled as she watched her disappear around the bend. That was one more reason she liked living on the beach. There were so many interesting people to meet. Last month Harry Turner and his wife had camped along the shore. They came every year on their vacation. Harry was convinced that the remains of a Spanish galleon lay buried somewhere in the sand with a cargo full of gold and jewels.

"They found beeswax on this beach," Mr. Turner said solemnly, "beeswax from India. It was very popular for making candles in Spain, and it would have been part of the cargo on one of their ships."

Mrs. Turner had pointed to the rocks extending into the ocean on the far side of the beach. "We

6

think the ship struck the rocks, maybe in a storm, and sank." Sam had shuddered then, gazing out over the rocks. For though she loved the ocean, it was a thing to fear when it pounded against the shore in a storm. She could almost picture the helpless Spanish sailors struggling in vain to reach land as the ship slowly sank among the rocks.

Mr. and Mrs. Turner had not found the ship this year, but they had promised to return the next and continue the search.

Sam shook aside her daydreams as she stopped to pet the blonde cocker spaniel tied to the end of the porch.

"Hello, Buffy," she said, smoothing down the dog's long, silky hair. "Looks like you need to be brushed. I'll be back, just as soon as I get dinner started."

Buffy rolled her eyes mournfully and rolled over for Sam to rub her belly. Until recently, Buffy had spent most of her time in the house. Now, she was forced to remain outside, because the man Sam's mother was dating was allergic to dogs.

"It isn't fair, is it Buffy? Mom ought to make Jim stay outside. You were here first."

Even before Sam opened the door, she knew her sister Julie was home. The radio was playing loud enough to knock the house off its stilts. It was a good thing their nearest neighbor was Mrs. Wilson. Anyone else would have complained long ago, Sam thought. Julie always turned it down before their mother got home, so Mrs. Tate never knew how loud Julie played it when she was at work. Sam would never tell, but sometimes she wished her mother would come home early just once and catch her. That would fix Little Miss Perfect. But it would probably never happen. Sam's mother worked until five, and then she picked up Kevin from his afterschool job. Officially, Sam was in charge until her mother got back, but since she was only one year older than Julie, her sister never bothered to do what she asked.

Sam smiled at the familiar cheerful jumble of furniture styles that decorated the house. It was a mixture of pieces from both houses, but somehow it went together in a comfortable way. "Early junk" their mother called it. Sam crossed the room quickly and snapped off the radio. Julie was in her normal position, stretched out on the floor, her feet propped up on a chair, with the phone glued to her ear.

"You'd better get your feet out of that chair before Mom get's home," she said crossly.

Julie made a face and stuck out her tongue, but she didn't move. Sam stomped to the kitchen, but a minute later she was back.

"You didn't do the breakfast dishes again," she yelled. "I have to start dinner, and the kitchen is a mess."

Julie ignored her. "It's just my witchy sister," she said into the phone as Sam glared at her. "I guess I will have to hang up." Still she talked for nearly five more minutes while Sam fumed in the kitchen stacking the morning dishes. It was Julie's job to do them before she left for school, but this was the third morning this week she had left them for Sam.

Julie strolled into the kitchen just as Sam finished.

"I would have done them if you had waited," she sniffed.

"Why didn't you do them this morning like you were supposed to?"

"I had to fix my hair. I was running late."

"You are always running late," Sam snorted. She snuck a look at Julie's long, blond hair. It fell in perfect waves nearly to her waist, framing an elfin face with incredibly blue eyes. It was no wonder everyone remarked on her beauty. She was gorgeous.

Sam's own hair was a murky brown. Whenever it grew past her collar, the ends became wispy and straggly. That was the reason she kept it short. Her own eyes were the same shade as Julie's, but on her they looked out of place.

"Help me peel these potatoes," Sam said. "I did your dishes. It's only fair."

"No one asked you to do them," Julie sneered as she left the room.

Sam was still irritated when her mother arrived home from work a few minutes later. Her brother Kevin was with her. He rode home with Mom from his job at the supermarket. He gave Sam a brief wave and headed for his room.

"The potatoes are peeled, and I put the pork chops in the pan," Sam said.

"Fine dear," Mom said absently. "Turn them on for me, will you? I have to hurry and change my clothes. Jim is taking me out to dinner tonight."

It sure is nice to be appreciated, Sam thought, staring after her mother. Samantha Tate. Sister to famous Kevin the boy genius and Julie the Gorgeous. Samantha Tate. Good for peeling potatoes and washing other people's breakfast dishes, but not much else. On a scale from one to ten she would be lucky to rate a big, fat zero.

Rats!

~

Meet me at lunch
very important!
Don't forget!!

Sam watched the note make its way slowly across the room to Sara's desk, keeping her fingers crossed that Mr. Ditmar wouldn't turn around and see. After Mr. Ditmar wrote the math assignment on the board, he drew a curled line underneath with a flourish. The note finally reached Sara just as the rest of the fifth-grade class moaned loudly. Sam grinned with relief. Alone in her room the night before, she had correctly guessed today's assignment. It was already done, put away neatly in her folder. Now she would have time for more important things.

She watched Sara open the note inside her book. Sara looked up and nodded, and Sam settled back in her chair. Mr. Ditmar was talking about science projects. Mr. Ditmar loved science. It was one of the reasons Sam liked him. Science was her favorite subject. The other reason was that he had never once said how pretty Julie was or how smart Kevin was either. Since he was new this year, he probably didn't even know them.

"I expect to see some really great work," he said. "You will have a month. That's when the Parent-Teachers' Meeting is, and I want to choose some projects to represent the class."

Mr. Ditmar would make a wonderful father, Sam thought. Having a teacher for a parent, especially one who liked you, could be a terrific advantage. Of course that was impossible, because her mother had not even met Mr. Ditmar. She wondered if he was allergic to anything. Definitely not, she decided. Mr. Ditmar was not the type.

When the bell rang, she hurried to catch Sara in the hall.

"What's so important?" Sara demanded.

"You've got to help me think of a plan," Sam said. "I was watching last night when Jim brought my mother home from a date." She paused dramatically. "It was awful."

"What was?" Sara asked as she unwrapped her sandwich.

"He was kissing her and hugging her," Sam said, making a retching noise.

12

"What's so terrible about that? He is her boy-friend, isn't he?" Sara said. "I think it's kind of romantic."

"That's easy for you to say," Sam retorted. "Your not the one who will end up with a father who sneezes everytime he's near an animal. Anyway, it's worse than that."

Sara looked interested. "What else?"

"Mom said his job only sent him here for a year. After that he has to go back to Ohio. And the year is almost up."

Sara looked at her. "Oh, no," she wailed. "You mean if your mother marries him, you will have to move?"

"Exactly. Now the question is, what are we going to do about it?"

"*We*? What can we do?"

"We can find my mother a new boyfriend, before it gets any more serious," Sam said. "Look. I've been making a list." She pulled a crumpled paper from her pocket and smoothed it on the table.

"Here are all the things I think a good boy-friend should be. Then all we have to do is select someone who has all these qualities:

Likes children
Has a good job
Smart
Handsome
Taller than Mom

Sara read the list out loud and nodded. That's

pretty good. But who do you know that fits the bill?''

Sam's eyes sparkled. "Well I thought about Mr. Breen, the mailman. He has a good job, and I don't think he's married. But he is probably too old." While she talked she added that he should be about 35 or 40 years old. "But then this morning while I was sitting in class, it hit me. I know someone who fits all these things."

"Who?" Sara demanded.

"Mr. Ditmar." Sam announced this so loudly that several people turned and looked at her.

"Tell me you are joking, please," Sara moaned.

"No really. Think about it. He must like kids— he's a teacher. He has a good job, he's smart, he's kind of handsome, he's taller than Mom, and he is just the right age. He's perfect," Sam said firmly.

"Even if he was, your mother doesn't even know him, does she?" Sara asked.

"No, but I have a plan," Sam said.

"Don't even tell me," Sara rolled her eyes. "I have a feeling I don't want to know."

"But this is perfect," Sam protested. "If I have the best science project, Mr. Ditmar will display it at the Parent-Teachers' Meeting. Mom will come, and she will meet Mr. Ditmar. He will tell her what a wonderful kid I am, and since all parents like to hear good things about their kids, it will be the start of a terrific romance."

Sara choked. "When you die you ought to will

14

your brain to science. Maybe they can figure out how it works."

"Are you going to help me or not?" Sam asked crossly.

"What do you want me to do?" Sara sighed.

"I figure I have to attack this problem from two directions," Sam said. "First, help me think of a really terrific science project. Then we have to think of a way to get rid of Jim."

"You know I hate science," groaned Sara. "But I guess we could do research in the library."

In spite of several afternoons spent combing the library for ideas, it was nearly a week later before Sam came up with one. Then it was quite by accident. It happened when she saw Harold Douglas sitting on the stone lion that decorated the steps leading to the school's front door.

Sitting on the stone lions was strictly forbidden by Mr. Foster, the principal. He was afraid they would break and somebody's parents would sue the school. Besides, he told everyone, the lions were antiques and ought to be preserved.

Actually, Sam thought they were rather ugly, but Mr. Foster gave a speech about them in assembly at the start of the school year. Hardly anyone paid attention, but Harold was not the type to break the rules.

Harold was sitting on the largest lion, with his chin in his hands, staring out into space. He looked the very picture of dejection.

"Why are you sitting there?" Sam asked. She sat down on one of the steps beside him.

Harold looked at her as though he was surprised anyone would ask. "It's Cynthia," he sighed after a minute.

"Who's Cynthia? Your girlfriend?" She could not quite picture Harold with a girlfriend, but you never can tell.

Harold looked at her disdainfully. "Of course not. Do you think I would be this upset over a girl? Cynthia is a rat. A white rat, to be exact. She had babies a couple of weeks ago, and my dad says if I don't get rid of them, he will. And he means it, too."

Sam shuddered as she imagined the fate of baby rats. "How many do you have?" she asked politely.

"Six," Harold sighed. "I've tried to find them a home. I've asked everyone. But all their parents say no."

"My mom wouldn't care, but her boyfriend is allergic to animal hair. It makes him sneeze."

Suddenly a terrific idea popped into her mind. "Rats are good for scientific experiments, aren't they?"

"Sure. Scientists use them all the time."

"Great," Sam smiled. "I'll take them."

Harold's glasses slipped off his nose in surprise. "All of them?" he asked incredulously.

"All of them. After all, parents can't stand in the way of science, can they?"

17

"Mine can," Harold said glumly.

"Well mine won't," Sam said firmly.

Harold looked at her suspiciously. "You won't hurt them?"

"Of course not," Sam said indignantly. "Do I look like the sort of person who would hurt baby rats?"

Harold gave her a careful glance. "No," he said finally. "But what about your mother's boyfriend? What are you going to do about that?"

"You let me worry about that," Sam grinned.

Sam was convinced that her idea was a good one, until the moment she actually stood with a box of scratching baby rats in her hand, ready to take them home. She had walked Harold home after school to pick them up. She was pleased with her good fortune—an experiment with real live rats was sure to be noticed.

"Are your parents home?" she asked. She watched Harold out of the corner of her eye as they walked. Although she had gone to school with him for the last two years, she had never gotten to know him well. Harold was quiet and always kept to himself.

"I don't think so," Harold shrugged. "My father left this morning on a business trip, and my mother goes to a lot of meetings. Our housekeeper is there," he added.

"You have a housekeeper?" Sam exclaimed.

"She's the reason I have to get rid of the rats. She said either they went or she did. Dad said it was easier to get a new kid than a new house-keeper. He's going to let me keep Cynthia, though."

"Where is the father rat?" Sam asked.

"He got out of the cage, and the dog ate him," Harold said with a sorrowful look.

Harold led Sam up the driveway to the biggest house she had ever seen. Mrs. Carson met them at the door. Sam could see instantly she was not the sort of person who would be fond of baby rats. She looked very stern: her body was tall and thin and her hair was tied back in a severe bun. She frowned when she saw Sam, but her face brightened when Harold explained the reason for her visit.

"Are you sure your parents will approve?" she said peering down at Sam.

"There is only my mother," Sam answered. She crossed her fingers behind her back, hoping it wasn't too far from the truth.

Mrs. Carson was so pleased with this news that she even offered to find a box so that Sam could carry them home. Sam followed Harold up a winding staircase to his room, marveling at how perfect everything was. Even in Harold's room nothing was out of place. It made you want to speak in whispers, like in a museum, and Sam was glad when she was once again outside and could take an easy breath. No wonder Harold kept to himself so much. He could never invite a friend to play in that house.

In spite of her confident air, Sam was nervous when she got back to her own house, carefully carrying the frantic baby rats. What if her mother made her get rid of them, before she even got her plan into action? Maybe it would be best not to mention them. At least, not right away. She made sure the lid was firmly in place and slid the box under her bed. She had managed to slip them past Julie, who was glued to the phone as usual. She knew she couldn't leave them under the bed for very long, but they would be safe until she thought of another hiding place.

She was still trying to decide what to do with them when Mom arrived home with Jim, whom she had invited to dinner. Kevin was with them, and he was talking seriously with Jim, asking his advice about what courses to take in his freshman year at college. It was easy for him to be friendly, Sam thought when she saw them. Kevin would be away at school. It was no problem to him who Mom might marry.

Julie tore herself away from the phone and ran to greet Jim. Sam frowned. It would help if Julie was on her side. But Julie was fond of the tall, slim man with an easy smile. Sam knew she would be delighted if he were to marry their mother.

Sam had made spaghetti sauce for dinner. It was the one thing she was allowed to cook, because her mother said Sam made it better than even she could. She used it as an excuse now, so she didn't have to greet Jim. She kept very busy stirring, and she added a little more oregano, though it didn't really need it.

"Anyone who doesn't like dogs can't be any good," she had told Sara after she had met Jim for the first time. "Probably, he secretly hates kids. He'll send us all to boarding school, just to get rid of us." She had known even then, from the way her mother's face lit up every time he called, that Mom considered Jim someone special.

"I thought you said he was allergic to dogs," Sara said. "He can't help that. My cousin is allergic to animals, and she loves them."

"Whose side are you on?" Sam had asked angrily. She had disliked Jim ever since she had learned he would be moving back to Ohio.

"Hmmm," Jim said now, sniffing at her pot of sauce. "Something smells mighty good. This daughter of yours is going to be as good a cook as you are." He put his arm around Mom as he spoke. "Maybe better. I might want to steal her away," he tried to joke.

Sam ignored him, in spite of her mother's pleading looks. He wasn't going to win her over with a couple of compliments. She grinned as Jim suddenly sneezed. It started slowly, but within a few minutes Jim's eyes were watering and the sneezes came one after another.

"Ah-choo. I can't imagine what brought this on. *Ah-choo,"* he said helplessly.

"Have you kids had Buffy in today?" Mom asked suspiciously.

"No," Sam answered truthfully. "I didn't." She felt a little pang of remorse as Jim's discomfort grew worse. She hadn't really meant to make him this miserable.

"*Ah-choo.* Maybe I had better leave," Jim said between sneezes. "*Ah-choo.* I'm not going to be very good company. *A-choo.*"

"I just don't understand," Mom said, looking bewildered. "What could be causing this?" Sam turned away guiltily as Jim slipped on his jacket.

"*Ah-choo.* I'll call you tomorrow," he was saying, when suddenly Julie screamed.

"A rat! I just saw a rat run past me."

Everyone froze as a baby rat skittered across the floor, and huddled in a ball in the corner.

"There's another one," Kevin yelled. He picked up the broom and started after the first rat.

"Wait. Don't hurt them!" Sam explained. "They are tame."

Her heart fell clear down to the bottom of her toes as everyone turned to stare at her.

"I think," Mom said grimly, "that you have a lot of explaining to do, young lady."

Spiders

~⁀~

"What happened then?" Sara asked. It was the next day, and Sara and Sam were eating lunch together in the cafeteria. They had invited Harold to sit with them.

"Kevin kept shaking his head, saying how dumb I was, and Jim kept sneezing. Mom made me catch them all and put them out in the garage. Then she made me vacuum the whole house, and we aired it out. Jim ended up staying after all, but the spaghetti sauce burned while we were catching the rats. It was a mess."

"Wow. What did your mother say?" Sara asked. She opened her tuna-fish sandwich and carefully picked out all the lettuce.

"Mom is so mad she won't even talk to me," Sam reported glumly.

"How did they get out?" Harold asked.

"I guess they chewed a hole in the box. Anyway, we finally caught them all."

"Is your mother going to let you keep the rats?" Harold asked with a worried look. "My parents won't let me take them back."

"Mom called the lady who runs the pet shop in town, and she said she would take them. Now I am right back where I started from. Worse. No scientific experiment, plus now everyone hates me and feels sorry for Jim."

"What did he say?" Sara asked.

"He was a pretty good sport," Sam admitted grudgingly. "After he got over the sneezing he laughed about it, and told Mom not to be too hard on me. But," she added defiantly. "I still don't like him."

Harold unwrapped several small cakes from his lunchbox and passed them around. They were beautifully decorated.

"They are too pretty to eat," Sam said. "What are they called?"

"Those are petit fours," Harold said. "Mom had some people over last night. I always get to eat the leftovers the next day. That's the only reason they are glad to have a son. They don't have to waste anything that way."

Sam looked up at Harold's slightly pudgy face. "You don't really think that, do you?"

Harold shrugged. "If it wasn't for that I would never see them. I'll bet they wouldn't even notice if I were gone. And Mrs. Carson would be glad."

"Maybe they are just busy," Sam said comfortingly, as she set the cake back down on the table. Suddenly it didn't seem so appetizing. "I'm sure they love you. Some people just don't show it very much."

"They don't," Harold said matter of factly. "I am just a bother they have to put up with. Someday I am going to get a boat and just sail away from here."

"You don't mind about the rats, do you?" Sam said, trying to change the subject. "I did promise to give them a good home."

Harold shook his head. "I'm just glad they are okay. Maybe I could help you with another science project. I am pretty good at science. I usually get an A."

"I can't think of anything else to do," Sam sighed. "I had it all figured out for the rats. I was going to give two of them a healthy diet. Two of them extra vitamins, and the other two a lot of junk food. It would have been terrific."

"That would have been a good project," Sara nodded. "I decided I was going to do one I found in the library. You give these plants some colored water. Then you can see it when it goes through the leaves."

"What am I going to do?" Sam wailed. "Do you know about anything except rats?"

25

"I'm doing mine on electricity," Harold said. "I'm going to build a capacitor."

"What is that?" Sam asked.

"It's something that stores up electric charges. Of course mine will be a pretty simple one, but I thought Dad would be interested. He's an electrical engineer."

"Is he helping you?" Sara asked.

"Well, he's been kind of busy lately," Harold sighed. "But he said he might in a few days," he added hopefully. He fell silent. Then suddenly he brightened. "I've got it. How about spiders?"

"Spiders?" Both Sam and Sara squealed at the same time.

"Spiders," Harold repeated. "There are a lot of them around, and I know a little bit about them."

Sara shivered. "I know a little bit about them, too. I know I hate them."

Sam was looking at Harold seriously. She wasn't crazy about them, but she wasn't afraid of them, either. "You know, that's a pretty good idea," she said. "Spiders might be kind of interesting. And I'll bet no one else would use them. But what would I do with them?"

Harold thought for a minute. Then he pushed his glasses up on his nose and leaned forward. "How about this? You could collect all the spiders in one place—say the school grounds. Identify them, make drawings of their webs. Stuff like that. Most spiders are really helpful, you know. There are only a few that are dangerous. Like the

26

black widow and the brown recluse."

"You wouldn't really do that, would you?" Sara moaned. Her face looked pale. "No don't tell me. You would."

"I think it's perfect," Sam nodded. "Maybe even better than the rats. I'll bet no one else will do anything like it."

"That's true," Sara nodded with a laugh. "No one else would be that weird."

"I wonder how many projects Mr. Ditmar will choose for the Parent-Teachers' Meeting," Sam mused. "I've just got to be one of them."

Marcia Stevens chose that moment to walk by and overheard. She stopped and looked at Sam with a superior air. "Mr. Ditmar picks one of the girls and one of the boys. Why are you so interested in Mr. Ditmar? Have you got a crush on him or something?"

Sam made a choking sound, but before she could think of a proper reply, Marcia had given her one last smug look and disappeared in the crowd of kids by the lunchroom door.

Marcia had been Sam's worst enemy since the first day Sam had started at Pinewood Elementary. They had both had a crush on a boy named Christopher James. Christopher had loved to eat, and both Sam and Marcia would bring him goodies from home everyday to try to win his affections. Marcia had finally won. Since her parents gave her an allowance, she was able to deliver a candy bar a day, pleasing Christopher's sweet tooth and buying his undying affection. It had done her little good, however. A month after school started, Christopher had moved, probably finding someone else to supply his treats. Sam figured Marcia should be glad—after all, she was saving a lot of money—but for some reason Marcia had never forgiven her.

"Don't pay any attention to her," Harold soothed. "But why are you so interested in Mr. Ditmar? You've been staring at him all week. Everyone's noticed."

"It's not for me, Harold. I'm doing this for my mom."

"Are you sure your mom can stand you doing all this for her?" Sara joked.

"Sometimes a mother just doesn't know what's good for her. That's why they have us kids—to help them with these little problems."

After stopping at the library, Sam headed home carrying three new books on spiders. Mrs. Wilson passed her as Sam was opening her back door.

"Looks as though you have a lot of homework tonight," she called as she headed for the beach path.

"I have to study for my science project," Sam called back.

"That is one subject I was never very good at when I was in school," Mrs. Wilson admitted.

"It's my favorite," Sam said. "I'm trying to have the best project in the class." Suddenly, she realized that was true. Even if her mother never met

Mr. Ditmar, she wanted to win, just for herself.

"Good luck," Mrs. Wilson smiled. "By the way, I have a new riddle for you: Look at my face, I am everybody/ Look at my back, I am nobody/ What am I?"

Sam thought for a minute, but she couldn't guess. "I give up," she said reluctantly.

"It's a mirror," Mrs. Wilson chuckled. "The lady in the beauty parlor told me that one." Everyone in the neighborhood knew how Mrs. Wilson loved riddles.

"You got me that time," Sam laughed. She waved as Mrs. Wilson continued down the path, then turned to go in the house. To her surprise, Julie was not on the phone. Even more surprising, Julie was in the kitchen, finishing the breakfast dishes.

Sam put her books on the table and read Mom's instructions for dinner. All that time Julie ignored her, never turning from the sink, although Sam knew Julie had heard her come in.

"That was an awfully mean thing you did to Jim last night," Julie said, finally turning to give Sam an angry look. "You knew he was allergic to animal fur."

Sam sighed. Until now she had been so busy with her plans for the project, she had forgotten the night before. She shrugged. "I forgot. It's not my fault he has allergies. Anyway, this is our house, not his. I don't see why I have to change my life, just for him. Who needs him anyway?"

"I like him," Julie sniffed.

"Hooray for you. That doesn't mean I have to. I wish he'd go back to Ohio where he came from."

Julie slammed the dishrag against the sink. "Don't you want to have a father? Ever since Dad died everything feels wrong. We hardly ever see Mom anymore. She's always working. And I hate it in school when you have to fill out those stupid forms. They always ask what your father does. I hate it."

Julie's eyes filled with angry tears, and for a minute Sam felt herself softening. Even though it had been three years since their father had been killed in a car accident, Sam still felt an aching emptiness. She knew exactly how Julie felt.

She touched Julie's arm gently. "It's the same with me. Really. I'd like a dad,too. But not him. I don't want to move."

"Even the kids whose parents are divorced at least get to see both of them. Jennifer Warren's parents are divorced, and her dad takes her places every weekend."

"I said I'd like to have a dad, too," Sam began. "But not Jim. If you would help me maybe we could find Mom a new boyfriend."

"You can't do that," Julie exclaimed.

"Why can't I?" Sam retorted.

"Because it's dumb. Mom loves Jim. She looks happier than she has been in years. I don't want to move either, but it would be worth it to have a father." She looked steadily at Sam. "You might

31

like him, too, if you would give him a chance. How can you even know what he's like? Everytime he comes you lock yourself in your room."

Sam turned away and busied herself peeling carrots. She had been about to explain her plans to Julie, but she could see her sister would never agree, no matter what. Julie liked Jim, and she would never understand about Mr. Ditmar. But Sam knew Julie would be all right when Mom fell for him. It would solve *all* their problems. Mom would have a husband, Julie would have a father, and Sam could stay right here where she belonged.

Julie drifted to the front room and sat watching television. Sam finished with the dinner preparations and hurried to change her clothes. She was meeting Sara and Harold at the beach. Harold was going to show them a boat his family owned. She peeked in at Julie before she left. For a second she was tempted to ask her if she wanted to go with them. Julie looked so alone sitting there. Then she shrugged. Julie had her own friends, and Sam had hers. It was better to leave it that way.

"I'll be back in about an hour," she called. Julie looked up but didn't answer as Sam walked out the door.

Harold and Sara were already waiting when she reached the rocks where they had agreed to meet. Harold jumped down from the rocks where he had been standing, letting the waves wash over the bottom of his pants. The beach was quite rough here, as the waves crashed into the giant rocks along the shore.

"You'd better be careful," Sam yelled over the pounding waves. Those rocks were slippery.

"Don't you love it?" Harold exclaimed exuberantly. "Someday I am going to get on a boat and sail all the way around the world." He waved his arms enthusiastically in the air.

Sara caught his mood. "I'm going to a big city. New York, or maybe Paris," she said dreamily.

"What are you going to do there?" Sam asked.

"I don't know yet. Something that will make me famous, and fabulously wealthy."

Sam watched a sand crab scurry to his hole. "You're both crazy. I'm going to stay right here."

"Maybe," Sara said darkly.

"No maybe about it." Sam frowned. They had walked around the cove as they talked. The ocean here was calmer, and the town of Glen Harbor stretched away from the beach. A small wharf was here, filled with boats. Many of them belonged to local fishermen, and there were a couple of charter boats for the tourists. Here and there a sleek, privately owned boat was tied among them. It was to the biggest of these that Harold led them. The name printed on the side was MARY ANN.

"That's my mother's name," Harold said as he helped them board.

"Are you sure your parents won't care if we are here?" Sam asked. She gazed with delight at the small neat cabin. A galley was at one end and

33

down a few steps were the sleeping berths.

Harold shrugged and sat at the table. To her alarm, Sam thought she saw a trace of tears in Harold's eyes.

"They sold it," Harold said bitterly. "The new owner is coming to pick it up in a few weeks. Dad promised we would take a real trip in it someday. But now he says he hasn't got time, and it is too expensive to keep up when we hardly ever use it."

"It's beautiful," Sam said. "I can see why you love it." She put her arm awkwardly around Harold's shoulders. "Maybe you and I can just live on the beach when we grow up," she tried to joke. "We could be beach bums or look for sunken ships like the Turners."

Harold grinned. "Sure. I could catch us some fish or we could eat sand crabs if we are hungry."

Sam laughed, too. "Uuck. We could build a house out of driftwood and have as many rats as we wanted."

"We could throw the bones out the window when we ate steak and make as much mess as we wanted. If we needed any money, we could just ask our rich and famous friend here," Harold said.

"You guys are crazy," Sara giggled. "We better get out of here. The boat doesn't really belong to you anymore. We might get in trouble if anyone saw us."

The smile faded from Harold's face, and he nodded. "I just wanted to show you before it was gone. I never showed it to anyone before."

"I'm glad you did, Harold," Sam said. "It's really a terrific boat." She looked at her watch. "I'd better get home before I'm late. I'm in enough hot water already."

Sam waved good-bye and walked down the beach alone. It was shorter for Sara and Harold to walk through town to their houses. She thought about Harold as she walked. It must be awful not to have anyone that you knew loved you. Even though her mother was often busy and tired when she came home from work, Sam had no doubts about how much she was loved. But poor Harold didn't seem to have anyone. Even Julie and Kevin, though they were sometimes a big pain, were a part of her, and though she didn't often admit it, she loved them, too. All the more reason why they didn't really need Jim.

We are a family, she told herself stubbornly. We don't need any outsider to come between us. We are doing just fine all by ourselves.

A Witch's Brew

~

"When do parents come to school?" Sam asked Sara.

"Is this one of your riddles?"

"No, I'm serious. When do parents come to school?' she repeated.

Sara hesitated. "If you get in trouble, or if you get sick."

"Exactly. And I think I will start with sick."

"What if they make you go to a doctor? Everyone would find out you are faking."

"Then I will really have to get sick," Sam said firmly. "At school, so Mom has to come and get me."

"I know I shouldn't ask, but just how are you going to arrange that?" Sara groaned.

36

"I thought about visiting Aaron Phelps. I heard he had the chicken pox. But I think maybe I had it when I was real young. Do you know anyone else who is sick with something interesting?"

"My little brother has diaper rash," Sara giggled. "But I don't suppose that's what you have in mind."

"Very funny." Sam grinned, too. "Now be serious. Do you know anyone who is sick?"

Sara shook her head, still giggling.

"Well, then I will have to make myself sick."

"How could you do that?" Sara stopped laughing long enough to ask.

"I could mix up a bunch of really awful things to drink. Something that would make me throw up."

"You are crazy. Do you know that?" Sara sighed. "You are going through all this, and you don't even know if your mother will like Mr. Ditmar when she meets him. Or if he will like her."

"Of course she will like him. Isn't Mr. Ditmar the nicest teacher we ever had? And how could anyone not like my Mom?"

When Sara nodded, Sam was encouraged. "Mr. Ditmar is pretty good looking, too. Of course he does have that little bald spot on top of his head, but a grown woman wouldn't care about a little thing like that, would she?"

"I didn't know he had a bald spot," Sara said giggling again.

"You can hardly see it because he combs his

hair over it. I had to check him out pretty carefully. After all, if he marries my mother he would
be my stepfather." Sam grinned. "Look the next
time he bends his head over. But that is the only
thing I could find wrong."

"Are you sure Ohio would be that awful?" Sara
asked. "Don't get me wrong, I'll miss you if you
go. But maybe you should just give up."

"There is no ocean in Ohio. And besides that
they have terrible winters with snow and cold. I
wouldn't mind a little bit, but months and
months? I'd freeze. And I wouldn't know anyone."

"You didn't know anyone when you came
here," Sara pointed out.

"That was different. I was kind of used to it because we came in the summer. And it is a lot easier to make friends when you are a little kid."

Just think about how awful it would be to move,
Sam reminded herself the next day. That way she
would have the courage to drink the small bottle
of ingredients she had mixed up the night before
and hidden in her lunch bag. It made her sick just
to look at it. Maybe it would be easier to just pretend. No, she told herself sternly. It would be
much more believable if she really was sick. Anyway, it couldn't hurt to have people feel sorry for
her. Mom was still a little annoyed with her. She
would drink it at lunch, she promised herself.

"You're really going to drink this mess?" Sara

exclaimed when she saw the bottle and it's sick-looking contents. "What is it?"

"I just put in a little bit of everything I could find in the kitchen," Sam assured her. "It's stuff like pickle juice and mustard and Worcestershire sauce. I figured all of them together would make me sick."

"It makes me sick just to look at it. How are you going to drink it?"

"I'll just hold my nose and close my eyes. You can't taste anything if you hold your nose," Sam said firmly.

"There is some white stuff floating on top," Sara shuddered.

Sam peered into the bottle. In spite of her intentions, it made her feel queasy just to look at it. "I think it's just some mayonnaise," she said weakly.

As soon as the lunch bell rang, she grabbed her sack and headed for the restroom. She washed her hands and combed her hair, stalling until the room was finally empty. It wouldn't do for anyone to see her. At last the last girl left, and the room was suddenly quiet.

"Here goes nothing," she said out loud. Grasping her nose between her fingers, she closed her eyes and drank quickly. Holding her nose worked, thankfully. She couldn't taste her terrible concoction, although several times something squishy slid down her throat. It's just the mayonnaise, she told herself, or maybe the peanut butter.

Opening her eyes with a shudder, she was startled to see someone had entered the room while she was drinking. The girl gave her a strange look, but didn't comment.

"I had to take some medicine," Sam explained, quickly rinsing the bottle. She tucked the bottle back in her lunch bag and hurried to meet her friends. Already, her stomach was doing queer little flip-flops. It's going to work, she thought gleefully.

By the time she slid into her seat beside Harold and Sara, she knew she was never going to be able to eat the ham-and-cheese sandwiches her Mother had packed, although they were her favorite. She pushed the sack towards Harold.

"Want to eat these? I'm not very hungry."

Harold looked at her with something like awe in his eyes. "You really did it? I wish I was like that."

"Like what?" Sara asked. "Crazy?"

"No. I mean Sam is doing something about her troubles. I wish I could do that." He slid some crackers over to Sam. "Want some of these?"

Sam felt her face growing hot. "What is that stuff on them?" she groaned.

"It's called guacamole dip," Harold said rather glumly. "It's pretty good. My Mom and Dad had company last night. I thought maybe Dad was going to help me with my project, but . . . "

Sam felt her stomach give one final protest. She jumped up, nearly flipping over her chair in her haste to leave the room. She nearly knocked over Mr. Ditmar as he entered the room, talking to another teacher. In spite of her misery, she almost smiled at his startled look. It was going to work, she told herself.

"I don't feel very well," she reported truthfully a few minutes later when she came back into the cafeteria.

Mr. Ditmar patted her back. "I can see that. Why don't I call your mother and see if she can pick you up?"

Sam smiled weakly. "Tell her I lost my lunch." It wasn't really a lie. She just wasn't saying what she really had for lunch.

"You go wait in class," Mr. Ditmar said. "I'll have the secretary call. Put your head on the desk, if you like."

Samantha did as he suggested. She was feeling terrible. But she managed a little triumphant wave at Sara when she came back from lunch with the rest of the class. "I'll bet she's faking," Marcia said in a loud whisper. Sam raised her head off the desk to glare, but even that was too much effort. Weakly, she lowered her head back to the desk. More and more she wished she had only pretended to be sick. Or better yet, thought of a completely different idea. It was hard to think with her stomach churning like it was.

Suddenly she remembered she was going to have to introduce her mother to Mr. Ditmar when she arrived. Everything could depend on those first few minutes. Maybe it would be love at first sight, she thought dreamily. She practiced introductions while she waited.

"Mom, this is Mr. Ditmar, the nicest teacher I've ever had."

No, not right.

"Mr. Ditmar, this is my mother. She is very interested in science, too."

That wasn't right either. It sounded kind of fake. Maybe it should just be simple. Mom, this is my favorite teacher, Mr. Ditmar. This is my mother, Helen Tate. There. Then she would leave them alone for a few minutes while she went to the restroom. That would give them a minute to discover each other. She could see it in her mind already. Mom would probably gasp as she looked in his eyes and realize that this was the man she had been waiting for. And Mr. Ditmar would take her hand tenderly. "I'm so glad to meet you at last," he would breathe.

Sam shifted uncomfortably in her seat. She wished her mother would hurry. Mr. Ditmar was already starting the social studies lesson. She had done too good a job with her mixture. She hadn't intended to feel this miserable. She had to keep reminding herself it was all for a good cause. Even so, she was feeling worse by the minute.

She had almost fallen asleep when she heard a tap on the door. Quickly she looked up. Now to put the plan into motion.

"I'm Jim Weirton," Jim's voice boomed in the

hall. Mrs. Tate was tied up at a meeting. I believe she told you I would be coming."

"Oh, yes, Mr. Weirton," Mr. Ditmar answered. "Mrs. Tate told me that when I called. It is nice of you to come. Here's our little Samantha," he said as he led Jim to Sam's desk. "I hope it is nothing serious."

Sam felt her heart drop clear down to her toes, right through her protesting stomach. How could Mom do this to her? She had gone through all that for nothing. Now everything was spoiled. She glared at Jim, wishing with a glance she could make him disappear. Jim put a comforting arm around her shoulder as she stood up, but she angrily shrugged it off.

"I hope you don't mind. Your mother called to see if I could come get you. She had some last minute papers she had to prepare for a court hearing. It happened that I wasn't busy."

From across the room she caught sight of Sara's sympathetic face. "I'm all right," she mumbled. "Maybe I should just stay here."

"Nonsense," Mr. Ditmar exclaimed. "You might be coming down with the flu. I wouldn't want you to give it to everyone in the class. And Mr. Weirton has come all this way to get you. You may as well go home and rest for the afternoon."

Without a word Sam gathered her things and followed Jim to the parking lot.

"Do you think it might have been something you ate?" Jim asked.

Samantha shrugged. "Maybe."

He felt her head. "You don't seem to have a fever."

She pulled away from him again. "I'm all right," she said shortly.

Jim took her shoulders and turned her around to face him. "Sam, I would like to be your friend, if you would let me."

"I've got enough friends," Sam said coldly.

"So many you can't squeeze in one more?" Jim said lightly.

"Are you going to marry my mother?"

Jim gave her a steady look. "We are talking about it, yes. I love your mother very much."

"She doesn't need you," Sam wailed. "We are happy just like we are. Right where we are."

"Are you afraid I will take your father's place? Because if that is what's bothering you, I won't. I mean I would like to be a father to you, but you could just think of me as a friend. Your sister and brother seem to like me," he added.

"Julie would like anyone. She just wants a father. And Kevin doesn't care, he's leaving anyway," Sam said cruelly. She jerked herself away and climbed into the car.

Jim followed with a sigh and started the engine. They rode all the way home without talking. Sam knew he was hurt, but she forced herself not to care. She huddled miserably on her side of the car. As soon as they pulled in the drive she ran into the house and up to her room, shutting the door firmly behind.

She could hear Jim dial the phone and a low murmured conversation. Probably telling Mom what she had said, she thought bitterly. Now she would be mad at her again. She lay on the bed and looked at the ceiling. It really had been nice of Jim to come to school and take her home. She supposed she should not have said those things to him, but she wasn't about to apologize. It was Mom she should be angry at. Shouldn't your child come before your job? she thought crossly.

After what seemed like a short time but was actually a few hours, Jim knocked on the door.

"Are you awake?" he called softly.

Sam realized that she had been asleep. She sat up slowly, surprised to find she was feeling better.

"I brought you some tea and toast," Jim said. "It might help." He sat a tray on her bedside table.

She discovered she was hungry after all. "Thanks," she said. She picked up the toast and nibbled hungrily.

"Feeling better?"

"Yes, thank you," Sam said stiffly.

"Good, I'm glad," Jim said awkwardly. "Look, I hope you won't be angry with your mom for not picking you up. She really couldn't get away, and she thought this might be a chance for us to get to know each other. I wouldn't want you thinking she didn't care. She was really quite concerned."

"I'm not a baby," Sam snorted, guiltily remembering her thoughts earlier. "I understand about work. It was just that I wanted her to meet Mr. Ditmar."

"Oh," Jim said. It seemed as though his clear gray eyes could see right through her. "Any particular reason you wanted her to meet him?"

"N-no," Sam stuttered. "I just like him. He's really a great teacher."

"He did seem quite nice," Jim agreed. "Well, I am sure they will meet another time."

"Are you going to tell Mom what I said?" Sam asked suddenly.

"No. I suppose you are at least partially right. It won't affect Kevin very much, and what you say about Julie may be true, although I would like to think she does really like me."

"She does," Sam mumbled. It was hard to dislike Jim when he was being so nice. But then a picture of Ohio crossed her mind, and she knew she couldn't let herself grow soft.

"I think I'll go back to sleep now," she said turning her back to him.

She felt him stare at her for a minute before he left and closed the door softly behind him.

By the time Mom got home from work, Sam was feeling fine, but her mother made her stay in bed. "Just in case," Mom said. "I felt terrible when I couldn't come and get you. I was so glad Jim could help." She leaned her head against his shoulder.

"I enjoyed it," Jim said. "It gave Sam and me a chance to know each other better."

"Jim even fixed dinner," Mom smiled up at

him. "Maybe we should keep him around."

"That's what I keep telling you," Jim said lightly.

Sam sighed, watching them. It looked like she had just made things worse. Mom would not meet Mr. Ditmar until the Parent-Teachers' meeting, and not even then if she didn't get started on her project. From the looks of things, that was going to be too late. She had to think of another plan. And it was going to have to be soon. From the way things were going, another month would find her living in Ohio.

Mom insisted she go to bed early that night, still afraid she might be coming down with something. But Sam had slept so long that afternoon she could not sleep. She sat at the window, staring at the ocean, visible in the moonlight, and listening to the gentle pounding of the surf. When she heard Mom coming, she jumped into bed and pretended she was already asleep. But the house had been dark for several hours before she finally drifted off.

Trouble

Just as Sam met Sara at school the next morning, Mr. Ditmar roared by in his little red sports car and pulled into the teachers' parking lot.

"Just think," Sam sighed wistfully. "If Mr. Ditmar was my Dad, I could ride to school in that every day. Marcia would be green with envy."

Mr. Ditmar stepped out of his car as they passed, looking handsome in his sport coat. "Hi, girls," he called. "I see you are feeling better," he said to Sam.

Sam nodded. "I guess it was just something I ate."

Beside her, Sara spluttered, trying to keep a straight face. Now that it was all over, even Sam felt like laughing. She had to be careful not to look at Sara, or she knew she would lose control.

Mr. Ditmar looked at her strangely. "Am I missing something? Some kind of a joke?"

"Sara's just in a good mood," Sam said quickly, glaring at her friend.

"You weren't faking yesterday, were you?" Mr. Ditmar asked suspiciously.

"Oh, no." Sam said it so earnestly that Mr. Ditmar had to believe her. "I was awfully sick."

Mr. Ditmar seemed satisfied with her answer. "All right. I'll see you two in class."

"You're a big help," Sam exclaimed when he was out of hearing.

"I'm sorry," Sara managed. It's just that when I think of you drinking all that terrible goo, all for nothing. It really is funny."

Sam grinned in spite of herself. "I guess it was pretty dumb. I'll never do anything like that again. But how could I have known my own mother would double-cross me like that?"

"You should have seen your face when Jim walked in," Sara said still laughing.

"Okay," Sam agreed. "It was a bad idea. But now you have to help me think of another idea."

"What do you mean? I thought you would give up after all that." The grin faded from Sara's face. "Anyway, that Jim seemed awfully nice. It really seemed like he cared about you."

"It's all an act. He doesn't care about me. Especially not now. And if he cared so much about me he wouldn't be making me move," she added.

Sara sighed. "What else can you do? You tried to get your mother to school and that didn't work."

"You remember the other day when I asked you how to get parents to school? You said get sick or get in trouble. Well getting sick didn't work. So now I'll try getting in trouble."

"Me and my big mouth," Sara said. "You'll have to count me out. My mom is already mad at me. Jeremy wrote all over two library books with felt markers and we had to pay for them. You'd think she would be mad at Jeremy, but no. It's my fault for leaving the books where he could get them."

"You don't have to get in trouble. Just help me think of something. Not anything really bad. Just enough for Mr. Ditmar to call my mom to school for a talk."

"There was a boy last year who stuffed the toilet full of paper towels and it flooded the boys restroom."

"I remember. But he got suspended for three days. I want to get in a little bit of trouble, not get murdered. That's what would happen if I did something like that."

The bell rang, and Sam hurried to her seat. "Try to think of something. Ask some other kids," Sam called over her shoulder.

By the end of the morning, Sam had collected ideas from several of her friends. Some she dismissed right away, like the suggestion that she set

51

off a firecracker in class. She didn't really want Mr. Ditmar angry, she decided. What she really needed was something to make him worried about her. She was carefully considering the last idea, sent to her in a note from Harold. She was holding the note inside her history book while she thought, and she wasn't even aware when Mr. Ditmar left the front of the room, until suddenly he was there beside her.

"Perhaps you would like to share that note with everyone," he said sternly.

"Not really," Sam pleaded. Across the room Marcia Stevens laughed out loud at her embarrassment, and Sam threw her a dirty look.

Mr. Ditmar stared down at her. "Read!" he glowered.

Sam stood up reluctantly. She read: "Don't do any homework for a week, and look sick every day in class. That way Mr. Ditmar will think you have troubles at home."

Fortunately, Harold had not signed the note. Mr. Ditmar stared at her for a minute. "Who is the note from?"

"I don't know. It just got passed to me," Sam lied.

"Why do you want me to think you have troubles?" Mr. Ditmar looked puzzled. When Sam didn't answer he said, "Perhaps you had better stay in during recess, and we will talk about this."

Somehow, Sam made it through the rest of the day, although she knew Mr. Ditmar was not satisfied with her excuse about writing a story for extra credit for English and collecting ideas from her friends. Mr. Ditmar had told her he would be looking forward to reading the story, so now she had all that extra homework.

When she got home from school, Julie was waiting for her. "I hear you got in trouble at school today," she said.

"Who told you that?"

"I have my ways." Julie gave her an infuriating smile and tossed back her hair.

"Well, smarty pants, you are wrong." Sam retorted.

"You had to stay in at recess," Julie said.

"I was talking to Mr. Ditmar about an extra assignment in English," Sam snorted. "So there. You don't know as much as you think you do. I'm trying to be Little Miss Perfect like you."

"At least I'm not weird. I don't sneak rats in the house and drink stuff to make me sick."

Sam had already started up the stairs to her room, but she stopped and turned back to stare at Julie. "Who told you that?" As soon as she said it, she remembered the girl who had come into the restroom while she was forcing down the mixture. Now she knew why the girl had looked so familiar. She was in Julie's class.

"I'm going to tell Mom what you are doing," Julie said.

"If you do I'll never speak to you again." Sam sputtered angrily.

"I suppose that's going to bother me?" Julie screamed back.

Sam stomped out of the house, letting the door slam. She plopped down the steps and stared out at the water. The waves were breaking in little white caps against the shore. She put her head on her hands and rested her elbows on her knees. Nothing was right anymore. Was it so terrible to want to stay in a place you loved? It seemed like the harder she tried, the madder everyone got at her. Angry tears washed over her eyes, and she roughly brushed at them with the back of her hand.

Mrs. Wilson trudged up the path from the beach, and Sam groaned. As much as she liked her, she was not in the mood for Mrs. Wilson's corny jokes. But it was too late for a graceful escape. Mrs. Wilson had already seen her.

"Mr. Zepata gave me a good one for you today," Mrs. Wilson said. "What is the most important use for cowhide?"

Mr. Zepata fixed shoes in a little store in the shopping center.

"Shoes?" Sam guessed knowing it was wrong.

"Nope. It holds the cow together." Mrs. Wilson laughed so hard that her stomach bounced up and down like jelly.

"That's a good one," Sam said dully.

"You look mighty down in the dumps today," Mrs. Wilson looked at her thoughtfully. Without

54

waiting for an answer, she eased her ample body down on the step beside Sam. "Can an old friend help?"

Sam shook her head, but then without really meaning to, she found herself pouring out her troubles.

"Well," Mrs. Wilson said when she was done. "That's quite a dilemma."

"Everyone is mad at me, and I don't know what else to do to make Mom stay here," Sam cried.

Mrs. Wilson put one of her big arms around Sam's shoulders. "It is very beautiful here," she said. "That's why I came here to paint. But there are a lot of other beautiful places in the world. Some of them I've seen, and some I'd like to before I die. But you know, it isn't really the place that makes us happy. I wonder how nice this place would be if you had three unhappy people around you. Sometimes, I think it is a good thing to work for what you want. But maybe other times, it is better to try to want what you get. Are you sure it is really moving you are afraid of?"

"I'm not afraid. I just like it here," Sam said stubbornly.

"Here where you have all your friends, and you have made a place for yourself? Perhaps you won't be so important when your mother doesn't need to rely on you so much after she's married. But perhaps that isn't why you are important in the first place. Why don't you take a chance and find out.

55

You know, Kevin may be awfully smart, and Julie is very pretty. But it is *you* I am friends with. I think you are a pretty special person."

Sam looked back over the ocean. Could Mrs. Wilson be right? Something told her that she was. Oh, she would miss the ocean if they moved, but most of all she was afraid she would lose the few people who thought she was special.

Mrs. Wilson gave her arm a squeeze and stood up. "You know everyone has something that makes them special. Look at me. I am old and fat. But my paintings make people happy, and that makes me happy, too."

Sam smiled up at her. "Mrs. Wilson," she said, standing. "I am glad you're my friend."

Mrs. Wilson beamed. "I can't help but wonder what you might do if you put all your energy somewhere else. She touched Sam's hair lightly. "And I think you would be an awfully pretty girl if you would fix yourself up a little."

"I'm not very good at hair," Sam said. "And I don't know what my specialty could be."

"Maybe your specialty is being Samantha Tate," Mrs. Wilson called back as she crossed the space between their houses. "I happen to think that is a very fine thing to be."

Love

~◦~

Sam was not sure how a person went about finding out what they were good at, but she did know a few things that definitely weren't her specialty. Playing the piano, for instance. Mom had started her with piano lessons when she was nine, but had given up by the time she was ten. That was when her teacher, an elderly lady named Mrs. Grundy, had come to the house and had a long talk with Mom. Sam had not been unhappy when the lessons ended. After a year, she was still struggling to learn the baby songs in the first book.

She had tried baton lessons and gymnastics with equally unhappy results. As a matter of fact, Sam couldn't think of anything she could do well.

Maybe she was the exception to the rule about everyone being good at something.

Mrs. Wilson was right about one thing though. Her plans for getting Mom together with Mr. Ditmar were hopeless. Mr. Ditmar called that very night, and had a long talk with Mom. When Mom got off the phone, she didn't look like a woman who had just been struck by love. She just looked like a woman who was very irritated with her daughter.

"Mr. Ditmar seems to think there is something bothering you. He says you have been acting strange lately, and he has the feeling you are trying to get yourself in trouble."

"Why would anyone want to get themselves in trouble?" Sam hedged.

"Suppose you tell me," Mom said sternly.

"I was just trying to think of a way for you to meet Mr. Ditmar," Sam confessed.

Mom looked confused. "I must have missed something. You wanted to get in trouble so I would meet your teacher?"

Sam nodded miserably. "I thought that if you met him you might like him better than Jim."

"Oh, honey," Mom said. "I didn't know you felt that way. Why didn't you just ask me to meet him?"

"I didn't think you would unless there was a really good reason. You are always so busy. You used to meet all my teachers, but now it seems like you are either working or out with Jim."

"I didn't know it meant that much to you," Mom said thoughtfully. "I really don't have much time when I am working, and you seemed to be doing so well. I guess I thought it wasn't necessary." She flushed. "Now I see why you thought about getting in trouble." She paused, putting her arm around Sam's shoulder. "You know, if Jim and I marry, I won't have to work full-time. I'll have more time to do these things."

Sam didn't answer, and after a minute Mom stood up with a sigh. "If you would just give Jim half a chance, you might like him," she said. "And after this, if there is anyone you want me to meet, just ask me."

Sam looked at the peanut-butter sandwich she had made before her mother entered the kitchen. Suddenly she was not very hungry. She went to her room and started on the stack of books about spiders that she had gathered.

Spiders are not true insects, she wrote in her notes. An insect has three body parts, but a spider has only two. An insect has six legs, a spider has eight. There are over 30,000 kinds of spiders, and only a few are harmful to man.

She was so interested in her reading, she didn't notice how much time had passed. She had even missed her favorite program on television and was surprised when her mother called up that it was time for bed. Reluctantly she put away her books. Even if her project was not the winner, she decided, spiders were very interesting.

Julie passed her door on her way to bed, and Sam called after her. "Julie, thanks for not telling Mom on me."

"I should have," Julie sniffed.

"Well you didn't, so thanks," Sam said stiffly. "I got in trouble anyway."

"I heard. You wanted Mom to like your teacher and break up with Jim."

"I sort of gave up on that idea," Sam grinned ruefully.

Julie looked at her for the first time. "Do you mean it?"

"I guess it was a dumb idea. See I had this list of what a good boyfriend for Mom would be. But I forgot the most important thing."

Julie came in her room and sat on the bed. "What's that?"

"Love. You don't stop loving one person and start loving another, just because someone else wants you to." Sam stared out of her window at the shore. The moon was shining brightly, making a delicate pattern on the waves washing over the beach. "I am going to hate leaving here—the ocean, all my friends."

Julie sighed. "You will make new ones. Everyone likes you."

"You are the one everyone likes," Sam said in surprise.

Julie shook her head. "No they don't. The boys I want to like me act like they are afraid of me, and the ones I don't like hang around and then the girls get mad. If I try to keep them away, everyone says I am stuck up.''

Sam turned away from the window and stared at her sister. It had never occurred to her that being pretty might have a bad side.

"I have always been jealous of you because you were pretty."

"I've always been jealous of you because everyone likes you," Julie laughed. "Besides, you are just as pretty as I am."

When Sam started to shake her head, Julie reached out and touched her hair. "Why don't you let me fix your hair? I'll show you."

Sam looked at her reflection in the mirror. "Do you really think so?"

"Let's get up a little bit early in the morning, and I'll fix it for you. I am pretty good at fixing hair."

Sam nodded. She had a feeling that it would really please Julie to do it, and besides she definitely needed some kind of help with her hair. Mark that down as one more talent she didn't have. "Okay," she agreed. "I'll set my clock."

"Good," Julie said. Her eyes lit up in a grin, and Sam wondered how she had ever hated her so much.

Mom hollered from the bottom of the stairs for them to get in bed, and Julie scurried to her own room, waving good night. Sam climbed in bed. She lay watching the moonlight flickering on the ceiling for a long time before she finally fell asleep.

Sam wasn't sure she had the courage to go to school the next morning. Julie had lent her a blouse to wear with her new jeans, a ruffled, silky one not at all like the plain shirts Sam usually wore. It seemed to go with her new hairdo, though, and looking in the mirror, Sam had almost felt like a different person. Even Kevin had whistled admiringly before he had run out to meet the friend who was driving him to school. She was afraid someone would laugh and spoil the whole day, but Sara had squealed with delight, and even Harold had exclaimed over the transformation. Several times Sam had caught Marcia Stevens staring at her like she couldn't believe her eyes. She was so happy over her new look she almost forgot about the science project but finally remembered at noon.

"Tomorrow is Saturday," she said cornering Sara and Harold. "How about helping me catch a few spiders?"

"I have to watch my little brother while Mom does her shopping," Sara said. Sam thought she sounded a little relieved.

"I can help," Harold offered.

"Thanks Harold. I decided I would catch them alive and put them in some big bottles with a few twigs. If I can get them to spin some webs, that will be more interesting, don't you think?"

"Then you will have to feed them," Sara said.

"We can catch flies and stuff," Sam replied.

"But I have to capture them soon, or I won't have time to identify them. Why don't you just bring your little brother along? Maybe he could play on the swings while we hunt."

Sara finally agreed, though not very happily. Sam was afraid she might change her mind, but she was waiting when Sam got to her house to meet her.

"Why, Sam," Mrs. Rubens exclaimed. "You look positively beautiful." With Julie's help, she had done her own hair in the same style that morning. Sam flushed, pleased with the compliment, as Mr. Rubens began to sing: "Curly Locks, Curly Locks, wilt thou be mine?"

"Hush," Mrs. Rubens chided her husband. "Can't you see we are embarrassing Sam? You do look very nice, though," she said to Sam.

Jeremy was sitting in his high chair happily tearing up pieces of toast and feeding them to the dog. Sara wiped his face and helped him put on his jacket for the morning was still foggy and cool.

"Don't get so busy with spiders that you forget about Jeremy," Mrs. Rubens told them. "He can be quite a handful at times."

"We will take good care of him," Sara and Sam promised.

"Hi, Sammy." Jeremy grinned happily. He gave her a wet, sloppy kiss on the cheek.

"Hi, Jeremy. Are you going to help me catch spiders?"

"Spi-er?"

"Bugs. We are going to catch bugs," Sara explained patiently. Sara brought a sack full of toy trucks to amuse Jeremy and Sam picked up the box of large canning jars she had borrowed from her mother. Sam doubted she would notice they were missing. Aside from a batch of boysenberry jam her mother had made from the buckets of large, juicy berries Sam and Julie had picked growing wild near the cove, her mother had not had time to can anything lately.

Harold had not arrived when they reached the school grounds, but they did not have to wait very long. In a few minutes Harold came trudging up the sidewalk with a box of extra bottles.

"I guess we're ready," Sam said, sitting Jeremy on a pile of sand to play with his cars. "Let's each take a jar and split up."

"Spi-er," Jeremy yelled. "Jeremy sees."

Sam rushed back to him, jar in hand. She looked to where he was pointing and laughed.

"No, Jeremy, that's an ant."

"Spi-er," Jeremy insisted.

Samantha scooped the ant up in the jar. "We can always feed it to the spiders," she explained. She smiled at Jeremy. "Thanks Jeremy, you are a big help."

Harold picked up a jar. "I'll look over in the weeds by the soccer field," he said. He headed to the back of the school property.

"I'll look in the bushes out front," Sam said. "Why don't you look around the building," she said to Sara.

Sara took Jeremy by the hand. "Come on Jeremy. We'll go look for more spiders."

Samantha checked the bushes and almost immediately found a small green spider. She clapped the lid over it and made a note in her book about the web and where it was found. Then she returned for a new jar.

"Samantha, come quick. I found a great big hairy one," Sara was yelling as Samantha got back to the playground. Sara was standing near the basement window well making a face.

With a stick, Sam coaxed it into the jar. "That's a wolf spider," she said with satisfaction. "I know that one from the books I've been studying."

Sara looked at the jar and shuddered. "Jeremy dropped his car in there or I wouldn't have seen it." She looked around, suddenly alarmed. While they had been involved with the spider, Jeremy had disappeared.

"See Jeremy," a small voice called.

"Oh, no," Sara groaned. There on the top rung of the monkey bars was Jeremy.

"Jeremy jump," he laughed.

Sara and Sam set off at a dead run, reaching the bars just as Jeremy made his leap. He landed hard on top of Sara, who fell into Sam, knocking them both to the ground. Sam, on the bottom of the pile, came out with a skinned elbow, but Jeremy landed on top of the pile, unhurt. He grinned wildly at Sam and his sister, both trying to calm racing hearts.

"Jeremy jump," he said proudly. "Fun. Jeremy do it again."

The Mystery Spider

~~

"That is quite a project you've got going in the garage," Jim said admiringly to Sam. "I can see you've put a lot of work into it."

Seven jars lined the workshop bench. Sam had placed dirt and twigs in each jar, and to her delight four of the spiders had already made new webs, using the twigs for support. She was sitting on the porch steps working on a poster showing the exact location where each of the spiders had been found. Another poster, almost finished, gave the names of the spiders and a few facts about them.

"I've found the names of all of them," she explained. "Except for this one." She pointed to a plump green spider busily encasing that morning's fly in its web. "I've looked at all the books in the library, and I still haven't found it."

Jim had been on his way home after a date with her mother, but he stopped to talk to Sam and go look into the jar.

"I know a man at the university who is an entomologist. That's a person who studies insects. Maybe if we had a picture of it I could ask him to identify it for us."

Samantha gave him a grateful glance. "That would be great," she said, a little surprised that he would want to help her after all the things she had said. "Maybe Mrs. Wilson could draw him for me."

"Okay." Jim smiled. "You get me a picture, and I will see what I can do."

"It's nice of you to help me," Samantha said to him before he left. Suddenly she felt uncomfortable remembering how she had tried to get rid of him just a few days before. She still wasn't ready to be friends with Jim, but she had all but given up her plan to get Mom together with Mr. Ditmar. If there had been any doubts in her mind that it was a dumb idea, they were ended that very morning. Mr. Ditmar had roared by as usual in his sports car. Only this time he was not alone. Sitting beside him was a spectacular-looking blond woman who looked about twenty years younger than Mr. Ditmar. Sam had stood watching in amazement as the woman had opened the passenger side door and slid out. She gave Mr. Ditmar a peck on his cheek and climbed into the driver's seat. She was wearing a pair of sandals with very high slender heels, making her already shapely legs look even better, and Sam wondered how she ever managed to fold them inside Mr. Ditmar's tiny car. But then, Mr. Ditmar managed, and he was also pretty tall.

"That's Mr. Ditmar's girlfriend," Marcia Stevens whispered as she passed.

"How do you know?" Sam asked. She was startled. The thought that Mr. Ditmar already had a girlfriend had never crossed her mind. She chided herself for being so stupid.

"My mother knows a woman who knows him," Marcia said importantly. "She says they are practically engaged, and his girlfriend is a lot younger than him. My mother says it's disgraceful," she added.

"Why is it your mother's business at all?" Sam snapped. She wasn't about to let Marcia know how dumb she felt.

Marcia gave her a dirty look and stomped into school. Sam watched as the woman waved and drove the car back onto the street. They must be very close if Mr. Ditmar lent her his car.

Mom was pretty, but she obviously wasn't Mr. Ditmar's type. So there went the very last shred of hope for that idea. Truthfully, she had to admit she was relieved. After her talk with Mrs. Wilson, she had watched her mother closely. It was true.

Whenever she was with Jim she looked a little happier. Even a brief conversation on the phone was enough to make Mom hum as she did her chores in the evening. She knew she didn't have the right to ruin that happiness, though it still broke her heart to think of moving.

After Sam had cleaned up the mess from painting her poster, she went to her room. Reaching up on her shelf, she picked out a small book of riddles from the row of books. It was a gift from Julie on her last birthday. It wouldn't hurt to have a joke for Mrs. Wilson when she asked her to make the drawing. She found one she liked and hurried next door with the jar holding the unknown spider.

Mrs. Wilson was weeding her garden when she arrived. Sam inhaled deeply. Mrs. Wilson's garden was as pretty as one of her pictures. Riots of red, gold, white, and purple flowers filled the small walled area. In the center was an ornamental bench placed along a flagstone walk. From inside it was easy to pretend you were in another world, one that was always bright and happy and never marred by troubles.

Mrs. Wilson rocked back on her heels and shaded the sun from her eyes as she looked at Sam.

"Samantha. What a nice surprise. I was just about to go in for a glass of lemonade. Care to join me?"

"That sounds nice," Sam replied. "I've got a riddle for you," she said as she followed her into the cool dark kitchen.

"Shoot."

"How many pieces of pizza can you eat on an empty stomach?" Sam asked.

Mrs. Wilson patted her plump stomach. "I could probably eat about six, but I am sure that isn't the answer," she chuckled. "How many?"

"Only one. After that your stomach isn't empty," Samantha told her.

"I should have guessed that one," Mrs. Wilson

said ruefully. "I must be slipping. I have one for you. Why did they bury George Washington in Mount Vernon?"

Sam shook her head.

"Because," Mrs. Wilson laughed, "he was dead."

They sat at the kitchen table sipping their lemonade. "Now tell me," Mrs. Wilson began, "why are you over here trying to butter me up with riddles? It couldn't have something to do with that jar you keep trying to hide, by any chance?"

Sam blushed and put the jar on the table. "I

found this spider for the science project I told you about. If you could draw a picture of it, Jim could take it to a friend of his who might be able to tell me what kind it is."

Mrs. Wilson raised an eyebrow at the mention of Jim's name, but she didn't comment. She looked in the jar and shivered. "I'm not very fond of insects, but I'll see what I can do."

"A spider isn't really an insect," Samantha told her while she gathered up supplies for the small studio off the kitchen. "It's an arachnid. That's the same family as scorpions and mites."

"Well that figures," Mrs. Wilson grinned. "To tell you the truth, I'm not crazy about scorpions and mites, either." She began to draw the spider while Sam watched in fascination as the drawing took shape. Mrs. Wilson drew the spider from several different angles.

"I wish I could draw like that," Sam said enviously.

"Remember what I said the other day. I have two talents. I can draw, and I make a mean glass of lemonade."

"It was good, Mrs. Wilson. And the picture is perfect. It looks just like the spider. Thanks."

"Anytime," she waved as Sam went back to her house.

Sara and Harold came over the next morning with a jar full of flies and assorted bugs for the spiders. Sam would not see Jim until that evening, but in the meantime she was working on the posters, adding more facts as she studied.

"This is Hilda," Sam said pointing to the green spider. "I thought she ought to have some kind of name."

"Hilda?" Sara giggled.

"Well look at her. Doesn't she look like a Hilda?"

"I guess she does," Sara said, still giggling. She peered into the jar. "I'm glad to know you Hilda. Here is a lovely breakfast for you. Fresh, delicious flies. I caught them myself, just this morning."

The girls dropped the insects into the jars and refastened the lids. Sam lined up the jars on the workbench and surveyed her project with pride. It was a good project; even if it didn't win, she had reason to be proud.

"How's your electricity project going?" she asked Harold. "Have you built the capacitor yet?"

Harold sighed deeply. "Yes, it's almost done, and now I have to write something about Michael Faraday. Then I'll be finished."

"Who's Michael Faraday?" Sam asked.

"He did a lot of early experiments with electricity. The capacitor's ability to store electricity is called capacitance, and the unit of capacitance is called a farad, in his honor."

"That sounds awfully complicated," Sam said.

"Not really. All I needed were blocks of wood, coffee-can lids, and some wire. The hardest part was explaining what it does. But that part's done," Harold said glumly.

"Then what is the matter?" Sam asked.

Harold shrugged his shoulders. "I was just thinking: Jim isn't even related to you, and he's doing all this to help. My own dad can't even take a minute to look at my project."

"Maybe they will come to the Parent-Teachers' meeting if you win," Sam said, trying to cheer him up.

"Maybe," Harold said doubtfully.

Sam shut the garage door and walked with her friends along the beach. Harold seemed to shake his dark mood as the day went by, and they spent some time searching for unusual shells.

"When I first moved here I collected boxes and boxes of shells. They were all so pretty, I wanted to save them all. Finally Mom made me get rid of most of them." Sam said. She climbed up on one of the biggest rocks, balancing carefully with her tennis shoes and letting the salty spray wash over her feet. "I wish I could discover that ship wreck the Turners are always searching for. We'd be rich, and we could live anywhere we wanted."

"Not a chance," Harold said, not completely over his glum mood. "You would have to have all kinds of equipment and divers to help you."

"I know," Sam said, holding her hands above her head. "But it's nice to think about. I wonder what people do for fun in Ohio?"

"Maybe they go out and watch the corn grow," Sara giggled.

"You really know how to make a person feel

better," Sam said. She jumped off the rock and back onto the sand.

"I'd better get back," Sam said. "I want to give that picture to Jim. She peered at Harold, reluctant to leave him in his unhappy mood.

"Are you okay now?" she asked him.

Harold gave her a thin smile. "Sure. Good old Harold is always all right, didn't you know?" With that he turned and stumbled off by himself up the path from the beach. Sam watched him, unable to decide if she should follow him or not. She turned hopelessly to Sara.

"He was like that when he came to my house. It's really bothering him that his dad isn't interested in his project."

Sam glanced back up at the path, but Harold had already disappeared from sight. Shaking her head, she waved at Sara and ran back to her own house. They had stayed too long at the beach, and Jim and her mother were just leaving the house when she reached home.

"There you are," Mom called. "Supper is in the oven, and Kevin is staying home with you two girls. He's in charge tonight."

"Wait," Sam called. "I want to give you the picture." She ran in the house and up the stairs two at a time to get the drawing out of her room.

"That's terrific," Jim nodded when she returned, panting, a second later. "I'll stop by and give it to Professor Dodd tonight. Maybe he can tell us something soon."

Sam smiled. "Thanks."

Jim ruffled her hair. "You should smile more often. It makes you very pretty."

Sam turned away in embarrassment, but as she did she caught sight of Buffy, tied to the end of the porch. Ignoring her mother's unhappy look, she asked gruffly, "Are you going to make us get rid of Buffy?"

Jim looked startled. "I wouldn't do that. I know how much she means to you. She will have to stay outside though. You've seen what happens when I get close to animals. But I will build her a nice warm house. I promise."

"Okay," Sam said reluctantly. "I guess that will be all right."

"Believe it or not, I really like dogs. I used to beg my parents to get one when I was a kid. But of course, they never could. I just have to like them from a distance. No one hates it half as much as I."

"I guess it would be awful," Sam agreed.

Jim climbed in the car next to her mother. He started the engine, and then rolled down the window. "I hear you like riddles. Do you know why the moron took his nose apart?"

"To see what made it run," they answered together.

80

Where Is Hilda?

"What are you going to do if you can't find out what kind of spider Hilda is?" Sara asked a few days later. The two girls were in the garage feeding the spiders.

"I don't know," Sam admitted. "Professor Dodd came over last night and took a bunch of pictures. He says I might have discovered a new kind of spider. One that has never been named or studied."

"That's so exciting," Sara squealed. "You'll be famous."

Sam blushed. "I don't know about the famous part. But it is kind of terrific, isn't it? If it is a new one, I can pick out a name."

"How about 'samous hildas,' " Sara joked. "That sounds kind of scientific."

The first drops of rain were falling when the girls left the garage. All morning the sky had been dark and dreary, and now the wind was picking up and the waves crashed over the rocks.

"I think we are going to have a cloudburst," Sara yelled. "I'd better get home." She turned and ran toward Seal Point. Sam ran up the steps to the house and caught sight of Buffy cowering under the porch. The dog whined and rolled her eyes. The porch was already wet because of the driving rain, although it normally stayed dry.

"Come on," Sam called, untying her. She ran with her dog to the garage. "You stay here," she comforted. "You'll be okay here."

Buffy gave her a grateful look and immediately curled up on an old rug on the floor. Sam latched the door firmly and ran back to the house. She had to bend low against the wind, which by now was quite strong. Bits of leaves and twigs filled the air, and someone's garbage can lid rolled noisily down the street. Sam glanced at the ocean as she ran, catching sight of Mrs. Wilson struggling to the top of the path. She could barely hear her faint cry over the pounding of the angry ocean. Sam ran to relieve Mrs. Wilson of her load of paints and easel, helping her to fight her way to the house.

"Oh, dear," Mrs. Wilson moaned. "I knew I should have come back sooner. But I wanted to catch the sky the way it was, all angry and dark." She looked sadly at the painting with its colors running slowly together. "Now it's ruined, I'm afraid."

Sam wished she could stay and comfort her friend, but she knew her mother would be frantic by now. "I'd better get home," she said. "I'm sorry about the painting."

"Of course, dear," Mrs. Wilson smiled. She seemed almost back to her old self. "Hurry now, before it gets worse. There will be other storms to paint."

By the time Sam reached her own house, her clothes were drenched and she was shivering with cold. Mom jerked open the door and pulled her inside the warm house.

"Where have you been?" she scolded. "Go take a good hot bath," she said without waiting for an answer.

A little while later, warmed by the bath and a change of clothing, Sam explained about Mrs. Wilson while she toweled her hair dry. Outside the winds had nearly reached gale force.

Mom peered anxiously out of the kitchen window. "We should lock Buffy in the garage for the night. Where is she?"

"I already did," Sam told her. "I put her in before I came in."

"She hasn't been fed yet, I'll bet," Mom said. "And this storm doesn't look like it's going to end very soon."

"I guess that means I'm elected," Kevin remarked as he entered the kitchen. He slipped into a raincoat while Mom mixed up Buffy's food. "I'll probably get pneumonia," he grouched.

A blast of wet air swept into the kitchen as Sam held open the door. She watched as he ran to the garage, balancing the bowls of food and water. Just as he reached the door and slipped inside the garage, the lights flickered once and went out, plunging the house in darkness.

"Julie," Mom called. "Get the candles. They are in the right-hand corner of the linen closet."

Julie had been in the living room watching television. Sam heard her grope her way along the hall and back to the kitchen. Mom got out the candleholders and put the lighted candles on the table.

"There, that's a little better," she said. "But it looks like cold sandwiches for dinner."

"The television said this was going to be a bad one," Julie said. "I heard the weather report just before the electricity went out."

Mom patted her shoulder. "Our old house has withstood a lot of storms. But this is the one reason I don't like living near the ocean. I'm not so sure I won't enjoy living on solid ground for a change."

"Ohio has tornadoes," Sam remarked. "And I like the ocean when it storms. It is so"—she paused looking for the right word—"wild, beautiful."

Mom started making sandwiches, while Sam

and Julie found a bowl of leftover potato salad in the refrigerator and set the table. Working by the dim light from the candles, they soon had a passable dinner on the table.

"This must have been what it was like in the old days," Julie said, dreamily watching the flickering shapes the candles threw on the wall. "I'll bet it was fun."

"You wouldn't think so if this was all you ever had," Mom said. "You would have already been in bed by now. Children usually went to bed right after dinner. I suppose it was too dark to do anything else."

"What happened to Kevin?" Sam asked suddenly. "He hasn't come back in."

As if in answer, the door burst open and Kevin came in. He was holding Buffy in his arms, and the rain ran off his coat with a steady plop, plop on the floor.

"For heaven sakes," Mom exclaimed. "Why did you bring the dog in? She would have been fine out there."

Buffy shook the rain off her fur and wagged her stubby tail in delight at being inside the house again.

"I had to bring her in," Kevin explained. He looked at Sam. "There was a little accident in the garage. I've got some bad news for you, Sam."

Sam stared at him with a sinking feeling in the bottom of her stomach. Somehow she didn't think she wanted to hear his news.

"What happened?" she asked.

"I guess Buffy got scared and tried to hide under the bench. But somehow she must have knocked it over. There is broken glass everywhere. I was afraid Buffy might get cut if I left her there."

Sam slowly lowered herself into one of the kitchen chairs. "My spiders?" she asked weakly.

Kevin gave her a pitying look. "Sorry, Sam. I didn't see any of them except for two that were in jars that didn't break somehow. But it was really too dark to look."

"All that work for nothing," Sam wailed.

"Maybe you could catch some more," Mom offered. "Tomorrow is only Saturday. You've got all weekend."

"It's too late. The spiders all have to be identified, and chances are all the webs would be washed away. There just isn't enough time."

"I could write a note to Mr. Ditmar explaining what happened," Mom said. "Perhaps he would give you a little more time."

"He is going to choose the ones for the Parent-Teachers' meeting on Monday," Sam said. "I wanted to be the girls' winner."

"I could help you look," Julie volunteered. "Maybe some of them are still in the garage."

"I thought you were scared to death of bugs," Sam said.

"I am," Julie grinned. "I didn't say I'd pick one up. But I can look."

"I guess I could help, too," Kevin said. "If we can't find any of those spiders, than at least we could try for some more. With all of us working together, maybe we can get you a passable project."

A sudden thought struck Sam, destroying the warm mood she was feeling at the unexpected offers of help. "Hilda," she cried. "Is she one of the ones that got loose?"

"Hilda?" Kevin and Julie echoed.

"That's what I call the spider with no name."

"Oh, boy. I've got a sister who names spiders. I used to think you were weird. Now I know it for sure."

An angry reply sprung to her lips, but the friendly look on Julie's face convinced Sam she was only teasing.

"I guess it does sound weird," Sam said. "But I had to call her something."

"Hilda's a dumb name for a spider," Kevin observed. "Why didn't you call it something spidery, like Fang or Creepy?"

"Hilda fits her," Sam said. "What am I going to do? Hilda would have made me famous. Professor Dodd is never going to forgive me."

"Maybe she was in one of the bottles that didn't break," Kevin said, trying to cheer her. "I really couldn't see that well. I don't know which ones are all right."

Sam felt her spirits rise a little. If she still had Hilda, and Kevin and Julie helped her find the others, she might still have a chance. She looked at her brother and sister gratefully. How could she have ever wished they didn't exist? Maybe they were a pain sometimes, but when you really needed them, they were there.

"It's settled then," Mom said. "First thing in the morning we will all check out the garage. Now come and eat your sandwiches, before they dry out."

"Why can't we go look right now?" Sam begged. "By morning, who knows where they might be."

"You couldn't see well enough to look now," her mother answered. "It is so dark you might accidently step on one."

Sam had to acknowledge the truth in what she said. It was useless to search before morning. Maybe the spiders would want to stay in the garage where it was dry. That is if Buffy or Kevin had not already stepped on them. She tried not to think about that as they ate and washed the dishes. Everyone kept up a running chatter, to help take her mind off the spiders, Sam realized. But though she tried to smile and join in, she couldn't help but worry.

A Television Star

~

In spite of the raging ocean practically at their door, and Sam's nagging worries about Hilda, the evening was almost a festive occasion. The family played a game of Monopoly by candlelight, and although Mom kept getting up and checking out the windows, it was clear the worst of the storm had already passed. It settled to a hard rain and sometime after nine o'clock the power was restored, although the telephone remained out most of the night. It was still too stormy to go out, and Mom insisted they wait until morning. They continued the game until Kevin, all his properties covered with hotels, had forced everyone out of the game, one by one.

"That boy is going to be a ruthless business tycoon someday," Mom joked. "Charging his own mother all that money to stay at his hotels. Sent his mother to the poorhouse. Shame."

Sam and Julie both had to laugh at that. Usually, when they played, their mother won, and she was ruthless as she collected the rents.

"Serves you right," Sam laughed. Her mother only *looked* innocent.

The game made the evening pass quickly, and it was late when they finally went to bed. Even so everyone was up early the next morning, ready for a spider hunt. Jim arrived just as they were going out the door, and when Mom explained, offered to help.

"I tried to call last night," he said. "But the phone was out. I thought I'd better come early and make sure you were all okay."

Mom smiled. "That's sweet of you. Is there much damage from the storm?"

"Not too bad. The beach is a mess and there are some trees down. But the weatherman thinks there is going to be more rain. The storm moved off to sea, but the wind currents could bring it back."

Sam glanced up at the sky, still dark and unfriendly.

"I hope you haven't lost Hilda," Jim smiled at Sam. "That's why I was calling last night. Professor Dodd would like to come and get the spider to study. He says he is positive you have found a new kind. That ought to give your project quite a boost."

Without a word Sam set off for the garage at a dead run, and jerked open the door. Stepping carefully over the broken glass, she picked up the remaining jars on the workbench. Please let Hilda be here, she silently wished. Even as she did, Sam knew she was gone.

"She's not there," Sam said as the others reached the garage. She started to slump against the workbench, but Jim grabbed her arm and pulled her away.

"I don't think you want to sit there," Jim said. He pointed to the bench. "Isn't that one of your friends?"

"Yes, it is," Sam shouted. She was suddenly cheered. If one could be found so easily, maybe the rest were still here. Scooping up the spider, she dropped him in a new jar.

"Let's spread out," Jim suggested. "And everyone be careful where you step. I'll sweep up this glass from the broken jars."

With renewed hope they began the search. The garage was seldom used except for storage, and since the car had not been in the garage, the job was easier. While Jim cleaned up the glass, Sam and Julie searched through boxes and old flower-pots. Kevin searched along the rafters, and Mom inspected walls and windows.

After an hour of searching, two more had been

found. Now only Hilda and one other were missing. Sam sagged against the wall, tired and discouraged.

"Well, kid," Kevin tried to joke. "It looks like you were almost famous."

"Thanks for helping, everyone," Sam said glumly. "But we might as well stop. The other ones must have got out of the garage."

"I wish I could help you some more," Kevin said sympathetically. "But I've got baseball practice in a few minutes."

Mom started back to the house with Julie and Sam. "Aren't you coming?" she asked Jim.

"You go on ahead and get your breakfast," he said. "I'll just look around a little more. You never can tell."

"We've looked everywhere," Sam said.

"We must have missed someplace," Jim said. "Wherever Hilda is." ·

"Well, you still have five spiders," Mom said. "And with all of your charts and everything, it is a good project."

Sam and Julie carried the five jars to the porch and added dirt and twigs for a natural setting. Then Sam went in the house for labels for the new jars.

"Sam, come quick!" Julie shouted from outside.

For one hopeful second, Sam thought Julie had found Hilda. But when she came back to the porch, Julie was pointing to a van just pulling into the driveway.

"It's the Channel Six news," she squealed. "Look, it says so on the side of the van."

"What would they be doing here?" Sam wondered out loud. "There isn't enough damage from the storm to have brought them."

"Maybe they heard about Hilda," Julie said excitedly.

"That's silly. How would they know that?" Sam put her hand to her mouth. "Oh, no. Professor Dodd must have told them." She looked helplessly at her mother, who had followed her out to the porch.

"You will have to go talk to them," Mom said. "Just explain it was the storm. Professor Dodd still has all those pictures, you know."

"They will think I am really dumb," Sam wailed. "I find a rare spider and then lose it."

"The storm was certainly not your fault," Mom said. "Just explain it to them."

Sam walked slowly out to meet the woman climbing down from the van. Sam recognized her from the evening news, and although the woman was not nearly as attractive as she appeared on television, her hair and makeup were flawless. Sam realized what she must look like, her hair and clothes streaked with dust and dirt from the garage, and tried to brush herself off.

"Are you Samantha Tate?" The woman smiled

95

brightly as she consulted a paper in her hand for Sam's name. Although she was smiling, she looked bored.

"Yes," Sam nodded, "but—"

"We've heard about your spider," the woman interrupted. "I'm Martha Thurman. The station sent me out here to talk with you. We thought it would make a good human interest story for tonight's news."

She waved to the man with a camera who was just getting out of the van, weighted down with equipment.

"Over here," Martha Thurman called. "This is the girl."

"I have to tell you," Sam began again, but it was obvious the woman wasn't listening.

"Have you ever been interviewed before? No, I don't suppose you have," Mrs. Thurman said without waiting for an answer. "Well, there is nothing to be nervous about. Try to pretend we are just having an ordinary conversation. Don't pay attention to all this equipment."

How was she supposed to do that? Sam wondered. She tried one more time. "Before you start—"

"Good evening," Mrs. Thurman said brightly into the camera. She had her back to Samantha and was talking into the camera. "Standing beside me is Samantha Tate. She is eleven years old and attends . . . what school do you go to, dear?"

"Pine Street Elementary," Sam said, "But I really should—"

Turning away again, Mrs. Thurman spoke to the camera. "While doing a science project for school, Samantha discovered a new kind of spider. One that has never before been studied or named. This fact was confirmed by Professor Dodd, at the state university, who plans to study the insect."

Sam tugged at the woman's shirt. Martha Thurman barely concealed her impatience.

"A spider isn't an insect," Sam explained. "It's an arachnid. An insect only has six legs."

"Thank you for the information," Mrs. Thurman said. She didn't look very grateful, however. In fact she looked very annoyed. "Anyway," she continued, "Samantha will have the honor of naming the new spider. Have you thought of a name?"

"I've been calling her Hilda," Sam spoke quickly. "But last night—"

"Hilda," Mrs. Thurman chuckled. "Isn't that cute! Now Samantha, how about letting us take a peek at Hilda?"

"That's what I've been trying to tell you," Samantha said. "Last night in the storm—" From the garage she noticed Jim frantically waving. He was holding a jar and pointing to it with a grin. Sam took the jar from him with a grateful sigh. She held it while the cameraman took a close up of Hilda sitting on a twig. Then as quickly as it

began, the interview was over. Martha Thurman and the man loaded the equipment in the van and were gone.

"You'll probably be on the six o'clock news," Mrs. Thurman said as they drove away. Sam had overheard her tell the cameraman that they were to interview the park commissioner next. Sam felt kind of sorry for the man, but then maybe Mrs. Thurman liked park commissioners. Maybe it was only kids and spiders she didn't care for.

As soon as the van left she ran shyly over to Jim. "Oh, thank you," she cried. "How did you find her?"

"I just asked myself where I would go if I was a spider," Jim winked. "And I answered that a nice dark box to crawl inside would be a good place. That's where she was. Down at the bottom of the box of old rags. I guess I am an expert on the way spiders think."

"I wonder if they do think about anything," Sam said looking at the recaptured spider. "You know, when I started this project, I just wanted to do something different than everyone else. But now I am really interested. Maybe I'll be an ento-mologist like Professor Dodd."

"Good," Jim grinned. "As far as I know I'm not allergic to bugs."

"I am," Julie groaned when she told her the same thing later in the day. "Please, promise me you won't keep them under your bed."

"I promise," Sam grinned.

At six o'clock the family was gathered around the television set to watch the news. Sam had called almost everyone she knew, and Mom and Julie had called the rest of the town. She wondered if Mr. Ditmar had heard the news and was watching. But a minute later, she was wishing she had kept her mouth closed. It was a strange feeling to be watching herself nervously stammering her answers. Especially when there was a big smudge of dirt on her nose, and something that looked an awful lot like a cobweb clinging to her hair. Martha Thurman appeared to be warm and friendly while she came across as a real dummy. Sam peeked around at the others in the room. Mom was beaming, and even Kevin and Julie seemed impressed. Of course, since they had never been on television, they thought it was great. Sam made herself a promise. If she became an entomologist when she grew up, she was never going to do anything to make herself famous. Never again did she want to be interviewed on TV.

"It was awful, wasn't it?" Sam said when it was over. Actually it had only lasted about two minutes, though it seemed like an hour.

"I thought you did very well," Jim said. He was staying for dinner, and for once Sam didn't mind. In fact, she was making her special spaghetti sauce for him. "Have you given any thought to a name yet?"

"I think Professor Dodd should think up a nice scientific name," Sam said. "After all, he is the one who is going to be studying her. But it would be neat if her common name was Hilda."

"I have a feeling Professor Dodd would be delighted with that arrangement. I'll bet people could get used to saying Hilda. After all there is a Brown Recluse and a Black Widow. Green Hilda has a nice ring to it."

"As long as we are all together," Mom said. "I would like to make an announcement. I don't suppose it is any surprise, but Jim and I have decided we are definitely getting married."

There was a second of silence, and Sam realized that everyone was looking at her, waiting for her reaction. She turned the thought over in her mind, surprised to find it didn't really make her unhappy.

"I'm glad," she said, almost meaning it.

Jim put his arm around all of them. "How could I resist?" he joked. "I get three beautiful girls and a genius, all in one shot."

And the Winner Is...

⟋⟍

Mr. Ditmar frowned as he walked past the tables of science projects neatly displayed along each wall of the class.

"I am very impressed," he said finally. "It seems I have a room full of scientific geniuses. How am I to choose?"

The class groaned with suspense, but Mr. Ditmar was taking his time. He looked at each one and made notes on the small pad he held in his hand.

Sam crossed her fingers. She had been so sure of her project when she arranged it on the table. But most of the other projects were just as good. She tried to convince herself it wasn't important so she wouldn't be disappointed if she lost. When she had arrived that morning, many of her friends had crowded around to see the spiders. Most had seen the news show and were impressed that she had been on TV. Mr. Ditmar hadn't mentioned the broadcast at all, and Sam wasn't sure he had even seen it.

"I am going to need a little longer to make my decision," Mr. Ditmar said finally. "I'll tell you the names of the winners before you leave today." He stopped by Harold's exhibit, and Sam's eyes moved to Harold's empty seat. Harold was not at school. It was the first time Sam could remember him being absent. He liked school better than home, and he never missed a day. Sam had seen Mrs. Carson deliver the project before school that morning, but she had left before Sam could ask about Harold. Sam had thought she looked upset. She planned to go to Harold's right after school. He must be very sick to miss school today.

"I saw you on TV last night," Marcia said at lunch. Her voice dripped with sweetness. "You looked awfully nervous."

"I was," Sam answered shortly.

"They should have given you time to practice," Marcia said. "You might have seemed more mature. And of course you could have dressed nicely and combed the spiderwebs out of your hair." She giggled to several other girls.

"I am sure you would have done much better," Sam answered just as sweetly. "Except for one problem."

"What's that?" Marcia asked sharply.

"No one would ever want to interview you in the first place, because you are too boring." Sam walked away before Marcia could reply.

"Did I look that awful?" Sam asked Sara. "Tell me the truth."

"Of course not, silly," Sara said. "Marcia is just jealous. You sure looked surprised when Jim showed you Hilda, though."

"I never thought I would see her again," Sam admitted. "If it wasn't for Jim, I wouldn't have."

"Do you like him now?"

"I guess I do. Maybe I did all along," she admitted. "But moving away seemed so awful. I still don't want to, but maybe it won't be so bad."

"We could write," Sara said. "You could be my pen pal. I'd like to have one anyway, and it would be a lot more fun with someone you know."

"I never thought of that," Sam said. "I guess that would be nice."

"Hey, look at that," Sara said suddenly. She pointed to the tall blond woman Sam had seen in Mr. Ditmar's car. She was just coming out of the classroom.

"What do you suppose she's doing here?" Sam wondered out loud.

"She's the biology teacher over at the high school," a boy standing in front of them said. "My sister has her."

"No wonder Mr. Ditmar likes her," Sam said. "You know how much he likes science."

"I'll bet she came to help him pick out a winner," Sara said.

Marcia walked by with another girl. "Some people really like to show off," she sniffed as she walked by.

"I'd like to put Hilda down her back," Sam said. "That way we could find out if she is poisonous."

"Who?" Sara giggled. "Hilda or Marcia?"

Sam laughed. "Marcia Stevens is the one person I'm not going to miss when we move."

The afternoon seemed to drag on forever, but finally, when no one could stand it a minute longer, Mr. Ditmar told them to close their books.

"I told you I would reach a decision by this afternoon," he said. "I have, but it was difficult. Both of these projects have won because they show a lot of imagination and work. The winners are Harold and Sam. I wish I could display all of them though, because they were all done very well."

Marcia turned in her seat and glared, but everyone else clapped and smiled. Sam looked at Harold's empty seat, and some of the joy of winning was lost. He should have been here to enjoy this moment. She waited for the bell to ring so she and Sara could go to his house with the news. But just before school let out, a note arrived from the office. Mr. Ditmar studied it for a second and seemed to think it over. Then he motioned for Sam to come to the desk.

"There is someone who would like to talk to you

in the office," he said. "The bell is about to ring, so take your books with you if you like."

Sam gathered up her books, wondering what it could be about, and hurried to Mr. Foster's office. A tall, slim man and an elegantly dressed woman were there talking to Mr. Foster. Sam didn't have to be introduced to know they were Harold's parents.

"You are a friend of Harold's?" the man asked.

Sam nodded, still unsure what this could be about.

"Harold has run away," Mr. Foster said. "We thought perhaps some of his friends might have an idea where he could be."

"I don't understand," the woman sobbed. "We give him everything. He has always been such a good boy. Never any trouble. You hardly know he's there."

Sam's eyes flashed. "That's just it," she said. "You don't know he is there." She knew she should stop, but she couldn't. "You say you give him everything. All he wanted was for you to pay attention to him. He was working so hard on his science project, and you didn't even look at it."

Harold's mother looked angry, but his father sat down heavily in a chair. "I never knew it was that important to him," he said. "I have been so busy trying to run my business, I guess I—"

"Do you know where he might be?" Mrs. Douglas interrupted. "He got up from the breakfast table this morning and ran out without a word. I can't imagine why he would do such a thing. He has always been such a sensible boy."

Sam shook her head. She couldn't think straight. It didn't seem possible that Harold would have done this. "I don't know," she whispered.

"We have to find him," Harold's mother said sharply. "There is another storm coming." She looked at Sam. "You wouldn't lie to protect him, would you?"

"I really don't know where he is," Sam said. "But I'll look."

"If you think of anything, let us know," Harold's father said. "And thank you for talking to us."

Sam stumbled out into the hall, still hardly able to believe it.

"Harold ran away," she said to Sara who was waiting in the hall. "His mother says he left after breakfast and didn't come to school."

"What?" Sara could not believe it either. She shook her head. "Where do you think he might have gone?"

"I don't know," Sam said as they started out of the school door. "Wait," she shouted. "I do know. Come on."

With Sara panting behind her Sam raced toward town. The sky was already dark and overcast as they ran through the small business area and headed for the docks.

"Where are we going?" Sara yelled, trying to keep up.

Sam paused long enough to catch her breath. "The boat. The *Mary Ann*. Remember how much he said he loved it? That's got to be where he is."

"Shouldn't we tell somebody?" Sara looked around, but there was no one they knew in sight.

"Let's find out if we are right first," Sam said. She walked down the docks to where the bigger boats were moored. They could see the *Mary Ann* heaving about in the rough water, but it looked deserted as they jumped aboard.

"Maybe I was wrong," Sam whispered. "It doesn't look like anyone is here."

"No you weren't," Sara said. She pointed down in the cabin, where Harold lay sleeping on the floor. They climbed down the steps and gently shook his shoulder.

The Happiest Kid in Ohio

~⌒~

"Harold," Sam said gently. "What are you doing here? Don't you know everyone is worried to death about you?"

Harold sat up and blinked. "Sam. What are you doing here?"

"I asked you first," Sam grinned. She and Sara sat down on the floor next to him. "Your mom and dad are really upset."

Hope sprang into Harold's eyes and then faded. "I'll bet. They probably haven't even noticed yet."

"They were at school today. That's how we knew you ran away. They looked pretty worried to me," Sam told him. "Why did you do it, anyway? You didn't even wait around to see if you won."

Harold shrugged. "I couldn't have won. I didn't take my project to school."

"Well, you did win," Sara said. "Mrs. Carson brought it this morning."

"Mrs. Carson?" Harold looked surprised. "Why would she do that?"

"Maybe she cares about you, too," Sam said a bit impatiently. "Maybe they all care. Some people just don't know how to show it. And anyway, did you ever tell them how you felt? We are your best friends, and you didn't tell us you were thinking about running away. Maybe you don't talk to people enough."

Harold sat silently, and Sam wondered if he was angry. But she had gone this far, she might as well finish what she had to say.

"It's like us. You and Sara and me. We are good friends. But we wouldn't be friends if I hadn't stopped to talk to you that day. I always thought you didn't want to be friends with anyone. Maybe your mom and dad don't pay attention to you, but maybe you never told them you were unhappy."

Sam took a gulp and looked at Sara. Harold continued to sit and stare at the floor. After a few minutes he looked up.

"Maybe you are right," he said slowly. "I guess I knew it was a dumb thing to do, running away like that. Did I really win?"

Sara nodded. "It was you and Sam. You have to go back, so you can get your award tonight. I'll bet

your mom and dad will go if you ask them."

Harold looked glum. "They're probably too mad to go now," he said.

"As a matter of fact, we wouldn't miss it for the world," Harold's father spoke from the dock. He held the rope for his wife, and they climbed aboard. Harold jumped up guiltily, but his father put his arm around him and smiled.

"How did you find me?" Harold stammered.

"It was the only other thing I could think of," Mr. Douglas explained. "I remembered how much the *Mary Ann* meant to you. Maybe selling her was another mistake."

Sam and Sara stood up. "We had better go," Sam said, suddenly feeling like an intruder. "Our parents are going to be worried about us. See you tonight," she waved at Harold.

"Anytime you want to come over, feel welcome," Mrs. Douglas said stiffly. Still, Sam knew that she meant it.

"We will," she promised, as they climbed back on the dock.

"Everything is fixed up between Harold and his parents," she told Mom later as they were getting ready for the meeting.

"People don't usually change that quick," Mom said. "But maybe things will start to be better from now on. I'm proud of you, Sam."

"I didn't do anything," Sam said, surprised. "Harold's parents would have found him anyway."

"I'm still proud of you," Mom smiled. "I hope this rain holds off until after the meeting," she said anxiously. "It is a bad night to have to be out. I suppose not very many people will go."

As it turned out, however, nearly the whole town was there. Many people had seen the news show, and Sam's project was surrounded all evening. In the background, Professor Dodd waited anxiously. He was taking Hilda to his laboratory as soon as the meeting was over.

"What are you going to do with the rest of the spiders?" Sara asked.

"I could take them," Harold offered.

"Oh, no, you don't," Mrs. Carson said in her prim way. "No spiders, or I quit."

"Now, Mrs. Carson," Mr. Douglas said firmly. "You are the best housekeeper we ever had, but it seems we have a budding scientist in the family. Perhaps we could strike a compromise. Harold could have the shed out back for things like that. We could fix it up, and he would have a place of his own, where he could make as much mess as he pleased."

Harold stared at his father in disbelief.

"Humph," Mrs. Carson snorted. "As long as they don't come in the house."

Sam smiled as she remembered Mrs. Carson's face that morning. She was not nearly as mean as she acted, Sam suspected.

"Good then," Mr. Douglas winked. "Let's go get some punch and take a closer look at our son's

115

project," he said to his wife.

Sam looked at her mother and Jim, standing with Mrs. Wilson. "Come on," she said. "I'll introduce you to Mr. Ditmar. You too, Mrs. Wilson."

"I tried to think of a riddle for this occasion," Mrs. Wilson said. "But I couldn't think of a one."

"I know one," Sam said. "Who is going to be the happiest kid in Ohio?" She took her mother by one arm, and Jim by the other. "Me," she sang out as they walked across the room.

Masterful mysteries
by

Phyllis Reynolds Naylor

Winner of the Edgar Allan Poe Award

NIGHT CRY
Scaredy-cat Ellen Stump <u>really</u> has something
to worry about when a suspicious stranger
starts hanging around her house just after a
local boy is kidnapped.

THE WITCH HERSELF
Lynn is terrified when her mother sets up an
office in the home of a dangerous witch!

THE WITCH'S SISTER
Lynn is convinced her sister, Judith, is a witch—
especially after she sees her conjure up a real
live boy from the middle of a lake!

WITCH WATER
Lynn and Mouse are off on another witch
hunt—only this time it's a spooky old neighbor
that they're after...

For a complete listing of these titles, plus many
more, write to us at the address below and we
will send you the Dell Home Library Catalog.

DELL HOME LIBRARY CATALOG
P.O. Box 1045
South Holland, Illinois 60473